Wuthering Heights

A Drama in Three Acts

by Randolph Carter

Based on the novel
by Emily Brontë

A SAMUEL FRENCH ACTING EDITION

SAMUEL FRENCH

FOUNDED 1830

New York Hollywood London Toronto

SAMUELFRENCH.COM

WUTHERING HEIGHTS

STORY OF THE PLAY

Adapted from the first part of Emily Brontë's great Nineteenth Century novel, the play, "Wuthering Heights" has as its romantic setting two neighboring estates of the English moorlands, and as its story, a strange passion between a man and a woman, which tragically involves four other people. Savagery, akin to the surrounding Yorkshire moors, dominates the family at Wuthering, where its cruel master, Hindley, the faithful servant, Ellen Dean, and Joseph, a harsh, fanatical old retainer, are all entangled in the emotional struggle between wilful, impulsive, young, self-tortured Catherine Ernshaw, mistress of the household, and sullen, handsome Heathcliff, adopted as a gypsy foundling and degraded to be a handyman about the estate. Although in love with each other, Catherine and Heathcliff are too affected by the storm-heated and electric atmosphere about them to be happy.

The Grange, beautiful manor across the moors, is given a rich if dull gentility by its squire, Edgar Linton, and his silly and romantic sister, Isabel, a kind of life for which Catherine longs. During a thunderstorm, and in a fit of temper against his degradation, Catherine angers Heathcliff by accepting Edgar's proposal of marriage. Heathcliff disappears in the storm, leaving Joseph to curse Wuthering as a house of death.

Years later Heathcliff returns and finds Catherine at the Grange, unhappy in her loveless marriage to Edgar. When Edgar, weak and stodgy, presides over the tea for the unwelcome guest, Catherine and Heathcliff discover that they are still in love with each other. With thoughts of revenge on Edgar, and to hurt Catherine, Heathcliff elopes with Isabel, now slavishly infatuated with him. Catherine falls ill at the Grange, and in a tenderly lyrical moment, reveals to Ellen that the love between her and Heathcliff is too mixed up with a miserable kind of hate ever to have happy consummation in this life.

Heathcliff succeeds in ruining Isabel's life by dragging her down to his own level at Wuthering, and in punishing the now insane Joseph. Catherine leaves her sick-bed, comes to Wuthering, and, realizing too late the futility and bitterness of their spite marriages, she and Heathcliff are planning to go away together, when Edgar arrives. After a quarrel between the two men, Catherine dies in Heathcliff's arms, fulfilling Joseph's prophecy that Wuthering is a house of death.

Copy of program of the first performance of
"Wuthering Heights" as produced at Longacre
Theatre, New York:

Robert Henderson and Harry Young

present

WUTHERING HEIGHTS

by

RANDOLPH CARTER

Based on the novel by Emily Brontë

The Production Staged and Designed by
Stewart Chaney

CAST
(In order of appearance)

ELLEN DEAN .... *Viola Roache*
JOSEPH .... *Francis Compton*
HEATHCLIFF .... *John Emery*
HINDLEY ERNSHAW .... *Robert Bartron*
CATHERINE ERNSHAW .... *Edith Barrett*
EDGAR LINTON .... *Sherling Oliver*
ISABEL LINTON .... *Peggy Converse*

The time is the end of the 18th Century.

ACT I

Wuthering Heights, on a summer night.

ACT II

SCENE I : *The Grange; an evening in autumn,
several years later.*

5

SCENE 2: *The same; morning, several weeks later.*
SCENE 3: *The same; midnight, a night in winter.*

ACT III

Wuthering Heights; morning, the following spring.

Photographs by Will Weissberg

DESCRIPTION OF CHARACTERS

ELLEN DEAN: *A strong, good-looking woman of about fifty.*

JOSEPH: *He is a sinewy, gnome-like old man, with small, cruel eyes. He scowls angrily and speaks in his harsh, Northern accent.*

HEATHCLIFF: *A rugged, well-built youth. He is rather ill-kept, and his thick, black hair falls uncombed over his forehead.*

HINDLEY *is about thirty. His face is both weak and cruel.*

CATHERINE ERNSHAW: *She is a beautiful girl, slight, graceful, but very spirited and proud.*

EDGAR LINTON: *He is an exceedingly handsome young man, slender, fair and immaculately dressed.*

ISABEL: *A commonplace though pretty girl.*

Wuthering Heights

ACT ONE

SCENE: *The living-room of Wuthering Heights. A summer evening. The first quarter of the Nineteenth Century.*

The ancient house is stoutly built of wood and stone and has the smooth, worndown look of a dwelling in which many have lived and died. A platform two steps up at back. A great fireplace, Left, ends the low, beamed room, and down Right is a narrow window set deep in the wall. Up Left, an arch gives access to the kitchen. Through this arch hanging copper saucepans, tankards and cabinet are visible. Up stage, Left Center, a narrow staircase ascends abruptly to the upper rooms. A wood closet under stairs. Up Right, a heavy door, leading outdoors. Another door Right end of back wall. Two or three rugs are scattered on the gray stone floor, and a large fur one lies before the hearth. The furniture is of oak; crude, highbacked chairs and a low table, all polished by long usage. Down Right is a chair, above it an oval table, bench and chair. Up Right, a chair. Against stairs, a drop-leaf table, and two chairs against stairs. There is a wooden settle for two with covering and pillows against Left of platform. A table and stool below fireplace. Some ugly-looking guns and old knives hang by the

*fireplace. Rows of pewter plate, against the back
wall, glow in the lamplight which illuminates
the room as the Curtain rises. Everything is
in order and spotlessly clean.*

AT RISE: ELLEN DEAN, *a strong, good-looking
woman of about fifty, is sweeping the hearth
with a small brush. She gathers the few ashes,
listens for a sound from upstairs, and then
calls:*

ELLEN. Catherine, can I help you?
CATHERINE. *(Upstairs)* No, you can't. And don't
bother me!
ELLEN. *(Deposits ashes, takes her knitting and
sinks into the settle. She knits and begins to sing
softly)*
    "O mother, mother, make my bed.
    O make it soft and narrow!
*(Her song is interrupted momentarily while she
counts stitches. She continues)*
    Since my love died for me today,
    I'll die for him tomorrow!"

(While ELLEN *sings,* JOSEPH, *carrying wood, enters
from Right. He is a sinewy, gnome-like old
man, with small, cruel eyes. He scowls angrily
and speaks in his harsh, Northern accent.)*

JOSEPH. Small wonder God don't blast this house!
ELLEN. And why, pray?
JOSEPH. *(Putting down logs at door)* Matters is
in a godless way when servants can sing songs and
ballads.
ELLEN. What should I sing, hymns? Oh, get on!
If you worked as hard as I, you'd have less time for
fault-finding. Where's Heathcliff? Doing your work,
I suppose!

JOSEPH. *(Crossing down Right)* The gypsy may be in hell for all I know— He's the most heathen soul in this house. God bear me witness, he's got a black heart—and only evil'll come o' him.

ELLEN. *(Knitting)* Nonsense! If Heathcliff's grown into a hard, surly boy, it's Master Hindley's fault—and yours. I used to rub oil on his back after you'd finished with him. I guess you wouldn't try to lay hands on him now though.

JOSEPH. It's God'll punish him now for the curse he's set on Wuthering.

ELLEN. *(Scornfully)* Curse on Wuthering!

JOSEPH. Yes—curse! I'se born an' bred on these moors, an' I knowed Wuthering Heights afore Master Ernshaw brought that ragged witch's child—

ELLEN. *(Wearily—she has often heard the story)* Ah, Joseph!

JOSEPH. *(Moving Center)* An' I was in this room when he brought it. *(Pointing)* It stood right there in the middle of the floor talking some gibberish none could understand, and starin' around, starin'— And since that night every storm that passes over north England breaks on these heights, and the firs on the ridge is bent like old hags. *(Lowering voice)* And ye know it's become a house of death. Mrs. Ernshaw—Jamie—and now the master! (ELLEN *is about to speak, but does not.)* 'Tis the Devil's work cause a witch's child was brought to Wuthering! *(Crosses back Right.)*

ELLEN. *(Uneasily)* Witch's child! Why, everyone knows that Master found Heathcliff in Liverpool—on the streets, starving. A poor little waif, indeed—not even able to speak English!

JOSEPH. That's it! He spoke a gibberish.

ELLEN. He was probably put off some foreign boat, poor boy.

JOSEPH. *(Sits bench Right)* That's what the

master said—God rest his soul!—but I know he found Heathcliff on the moors.

ELLEN. *(Throwing down her knitting)* Oh, get about your prayers! I've no time to listen to your nonsense. And mind the room. Young Linton's coming to see Cathy tonight, and the place must look neat.

JOSEPH. He is, is he? Cathy's a wild, wicked girl. Her father no but burried and she's a'larking! She sh'ud be thinking on her soul.

ELLEN. Time enough for that!—She's got the prettiest face in the parish.

JOSEPH. *(Rolling out the words with relish)* "The lips of woman drip as a honeycomb, and her mouth is smoother than oil—but her feet go down to death: her steps take hold on hell—"

(HEATHCLIFF, *a rugged, well-built youth, enters Right. He is rather ill-kept, and his thick, black hair falls uncombed over his forehead. A silence falls.*)

HEATHCLIFF. *(Center)* Where's Cathy, Nell?

ELLEN. She's upstairs.

JOSEPH. She's prettyin' up fer young Master Linton.

HEATHCLIFF. *(To* ELLEN*)* Linton's not coming *tonight,* is he?

ELLEN. *(Hesitating)* Yes—he is.

JOSEPH. Didn't she tell you he was comin'? We all knowed it. Funny she didn't tell you—used to tell you everything. When you was children you was as close as two peas.

HEATHCLIFF. *(Hotly)* Why should she tell me? I didn't ask.

JOSEPH. Now she's a young lady an' lookin' somethin' higher than a gypsy. A young squire's more to her taste—an' she's out to catch him with her wiles, just like a harlot.

HEATHCLIFF. *(Crossing to* JOSEPH*)* Shut your filthy mouth.

ELLEN. *(Rising)* Heathcliff!

HEATHCLIFF. Take care what you say of Cathy or I'll—

ELLEN. *(Restraining him)* Heathcliff!

HEATHCLIFF. *(Crossing Left)* All right, Nell— I wouldn't touch him. Only when he speaks so of Cathy, I can't be silent.

ELLEN. Get out, Joseph, and leave us alone.

JOSEPH. In God's name—

ELLEN. You use God's name to cover a lot of mischief.

HEATHCLIFF. Oh, let the old devil alone, Nell.

HINDLEY. *(As he opens door Right. He is drunk, and not entirely coherent)* Heathcliff! Where is that boy? (HINDLEY *is about thirty. His face is both weak and cruel)* Oh! *(Seeing* HEATHCLIFF*)* Well, what are you standing there for? When I come home I expect to find you in the stable—in the stable—waiting to take my horse—do you hear? *(He staggers. Turns upstage; throws down cloak.)*

HEATHCLIFF. I hear.

ELLEN. *(To* JOSEPH*)* Joseph, get him upstairs and to bed. I'll bring some supper directly.

HINDLEY. *(Center)* To take my horse and rub her down till her hide shines—shines like the leather of this boot!

JOSEPH. *(Crossing to* HINDLEY*)* You waste words on the likes of him, Master. Small work he'll ever do, though the Lord himself order it.

HINDLEY. By God, he'll work or I'll turn him out—not even Cathy'll keep me from it!

ELLEN. You'll do nothing of the kind. What with your drink and Joseph's scriptures the place would tumble to ruin but for Heathcliff.

JOSEPH. In league with him you are—in league with the devil—the two of you!

HINDLEY. *(Starting upstairs)* Never mind 'em. The brandy, Joseph.

(JOSEPH *jumps to carry out the master's command.* ELLEN *stops him.*)

ELLEN. No.

JOSEPH. You heard the master's orders.

ELLEN. No. It'll be the death of him!

HINDLEY. *(On stairs)* Ellen—since fate has decreed that I live out my days on these Godforsaken heights, please permit me to shorten them by one glass of brandy.

ELLEN. But, Master Hindley—

(HEATHCLIFF *crosses, gets brandy from mantel, and gives bottle to* HINDLEY.)

HINDLEY. *(Ironically)* Come, Joseph—we'll drink to my hearty damnation. *(Exits upstairs.)*

JOSEPH. *(Following—to* HEATHCLIFF*)* You heard the master's orders.

HEATHCLIFF. What orders?

JOSEPH. To tend the mare.

HEATHCLIFF. *(At foot of stairs)* I'll tend the mare, but you, Joseph, had best watch out.

JOSEPH. Watch out?

HEATHCLIFF. Yes. Watch out or I'll lay a curse on you.

JOSEPH. *(Terrified)* A curse!

HEATHCLIFF. I'm a witch's bastard, aren't I?

(JOSEPH, *terrified, exits upstairs.*)

ELLEN. The master will kill himself with drink. You were wrong to give him the brandy.

HEATHCLIFF. He'd have had it anyway.

ELLEN. And you should know better than to frighten Joseph that way. You know he's sly.

HEATHCLIFF. *(Crossing down Right)* Oh, he can't hurt me any more. I'm too strong now, and I'll wager he's sorry.

ELLEN. Sorry?

HEATHCLIFF. Yes. He used to like to beat me, and you know it.

ELLEN. *(Is busy with tray, napkins, and dishes at cabinet, in preparation for* HINDLEY'S *supper)* I'm sure that's not so. He just thought he was doing his duty. You would never put your scriptures to heart.

HEATCLIFF. Nor would Cathy.

ELLEN. You were both wicked—and you banded together.

HEATHCLIFF. *(Sits above table Right. Laughing)* Do you remember the day we kicked the Good Book into the dog kennel?

ELLEN. It was a shocking thing—and on a Sunday too! You both deserved what you got.

HEATHCLIFF. No, we didn't. No one had the right to make us read the Bible if we didn't wish to.

ELLEN. Well, that may be your opinion, but you got a thrashing just the same.

HEATHCLIFF. *(Softly)* Yes—that was the time Hindley had Joseph tie me up in the barn and use the whip—a hundred strikes it must have been—till I was bloody— And him there yellin' about God and sweatin'— That's what I meant when I said he liked to do it. *(A pause, bitterly. He rises)* I hate him. I wish I was a witch's bastard so I could put a curse on him.

ELLEN. You should learn to forgive—you'd be happier.

HEATHCLIFF. I don't want to forgive. I want to

pay Joseph back. I don't care how long I wait, if I can only do it at last.

ELLEN. Shame! It is for God to punish wicked people.

HEATHCLIFF. No, God won't have the satisfaction— I will—when I find a way. When he used to beat me, I'd plan out how I could punish him—and while I was thinking about that I didn't feel pain.

ELLEN. *(After a pause—watching* HEATHCLIFF *closely)* Sometimes I think Joseph's right.

HEATHCLIFF. About what?

ELLEN. The witch.

(HEATHCLIFF *laughs shortly, then a silence falls. He takes an apple from fruit basket on the table and throws himself down on the hearth rug.* ELLEN *watches him for a moment.* JOSEPH *re-enters from stairs.* ELLEN *crosses up Left toward kitchen.)*

ELLEN. I've supper all ready for the master. You can take it up to him in two minutes.

(JOSEPH *picks up the logs which he left by the door at his first entrance, and moves down toward* HEATHCLIFF.)

HEATHCLIFF. *(Laughing)* Wood! Why're you bringing wood on such a hot night?

JOSEPH. Should I ask you what I can do?

HEATHCLIFF. It's funny to see you do anything.

JOSEPH. God'll bear witness I do ten men's work.

HEATHCLIFF. *(Turning away)* Then God lies.

JOSEPH. Blasphemer! "Oh, keep not thy silence, O God! Let them become as dung for the earth! Persecute them with thy tempest and make them afraid—" *(Frenzied,* JOSEPH *seizes a log and brings it down across* HEATHCLIFF's *shoulders.* HEATH-

CLIFF *cries out in surprise and pain and strikes at him*. JOSEPH, *however, laughing wildly, jumps out of reach.)*

HEATHCLIFF. You dirty sneak— I'll— *(He breaks into a fit of coughing and sinks back on steps.)*

(CATHERINE ERNSHAW *appears on the landing. She is a beautiful girl, slight, graceful, but very spirited and proud. She is dressed in her finest gown; and her dark hair is caught lightly at the nape of her neck.)*

CATHERINE. *(Alarmed)* What happened? *(Seeing* HEATHCLIFF, *she cries out and runs down the stairs to him.* ELLEN *enters from kitchen.)* Dearest! Are you hurt? What happened? Heathcliff!

HEATHCLIFF. Nothing happened. I'm not hurt.

ELLEN. *(Accusingly)* Joseph.

JOSEPH. I'se done nothing. I stumbled and a log fell on him.

CATHERINE. *(Turning on him)* Oh, you stumbled, did you? I know your sneaky tricks—you did it on purpose. You leave Heathcliff alone or I'll turn you out. I'm mistress here now and you'll obey me.

JOSEPH. You'd not dare turn me out.

CATHERINE. And why not?

JOSEPH. Your father said I was to stay.

CATHERINE. He's dead, isn't he? Who's to make me obey him?

JOSEPH. Hindley'll make you!

CATHERINE. I'm not afraid of Hindley! Don't you ever lift a hand against Heathcliff or I'll tell him to kill you. He ought to knock you down, and he would if you weren't so old. He won't hit you, but I'm a girl and I will! *(She strikes at him wildly.)*

HEATHCLIFF. Cathy!

ELLEN. Why, Catherine!

(JOSEPH *hollers, and as* ELLEN *pulls* CATHERINE *away from him,* CATHERINE *bursts into angry tears.*)

JOSEPH. *(Retreating)* And the Lord said—
CATHERINE. *(Screaming)* Who cares what the Lord said! Oh, get out! Get out! Get out! *(Drives* JOSEPH *out Right.)*
ELLEN. Cathy, please, child!
CATHERINE. *(Pushing her away)* Leave me alone —all of you—leave me alone! Look at my dress— and Edgar coming! What a house to live in! It's like a den of beasts. *(To* HEATHCLIFF) Get off the floor and pick up that wood. You're not hurt.
ELLEN. Such tempers are bad for the complexion, Cathy.
CATHERINE. Damn complexions! Damn Wuthering! Damn everything!
HEATHCLIFF. Cathy, I'm sorry.
CATHERINE. *(Center)* How dirty you are! Don't you ever wash? If you'd at least comb your hair you wouldn't look so disgusting. Can't you do anything but lie on the floor like a dog and fight with Joseph and sulk? *(Her voice breaking—crossing up toward stairs)* Oh, I'm miserable—my evening's spoiled— I can't see Edgar now! Ellen, when Mr. Linton calls, tell him I'm ill. I shan't see him. I'm going right up to bed, and I hate you both. *(She bursts into tears and runs upstairs. A silence falls.)*
ELLEN. Are you all right?
HEATHCLIFF. *(Rising)* Yes. It hurt for a minute, but I don't feel it now.
ELLEN. *(Looking toward stairs)* Well, I think Catherine is the most selfish, ill-natured child!
HEATHCLIFF. No, she's not—she's right. This isn't a nice house for a young lady to live in. We're rude.
ELLEN. I won't say who's the rudest.

HEATHCLIFF. *(Straightening the logs)* Anyway, I'm glad she's not going to see Linton.

CATHERINE. *(Re-appears on the landing. Her manner is cold and majestic)* Ellen, when Mr. Linton arrives, tell him to wait. I have decided to receive him.

HEATHCLIFF. But, Cathy—

(CATHERINE *disappears without a word.)*

ELLEN. *(Shrugging)* I'm not surprised.

(ELLEN *goes into the kitchen and returns with a bright cloth and dainty napkins. She spreads the cloth on the table up Center.* HEATHCLIFF, *who has finished with the wood at hearth, hovers about her during this and other preparations for the guest.)*

HEATHLIFF. Nell—

ELLEN. *(Absently)* Yes.

HEATHCLIFF. *(Forcing himself to speak)* Nell, listen— Make me decent— I'm going to be good.

ELLEN. High time, but the wrong time. I'm busy.

HEATHCLIFF. Tell me what I must do to have Cathy—to have her—admire me.

ELLEN. *(Ceasing her work a moment)* Cathy loves you.

HEATHCLIFF. You think so?

ELLEN. I'm sure of it.

HEATHCLIFF. I wish she did. She's wonderful, isn't she? She's superior to everyone on earth, don't you think?

ELLEN. I don't know everyone on earth.

HEATHCLIFF. She is anyhow. I wish she didn't like Linton.

ELLEN. Linton's a gentleman.

HEATHCLIFF. *(After a slight pause)* Make me one, Nelly.

ELLEN. *(Laughing)* All right—come over here. *(She takes him to the hearth where there are kettles, bowls, etc.)* You start with soap and plenty of water—and you must use them in the right places. Now, down on your knees! (HEATHCLIFF *kneels and* ELLEN *proceeds to wash his face thoroughly with a rag)* A gentleman washes deep—not only the edges, but the holes and corners as well.

HEATHCLIFF. *(Gasping)* Ouch!

ELLEN. Hold still! Hmmm—had I time I'd fix you so Edgar'd look a doll beside you. He does anyway. *(Looking at him)* I'll be bound you're taller, and twice as broad across the shoulders. You could knock him down in a twinkling.

HEATHCLIFF. If I knocked him down twenty times, it wouldn't make him less handsome.

ELLEN. *(Dryly)* It might. Now hurry—wash your hands.

HEATHCLIFF. *(Washing his hands)* If I had light hair and was dressed and behaved as well—and had a chance of being as rich as he—

ELLEN. And sat at home all day for a shower of rain! Oh, Heathcliff, you're showing poor spirit. *(Turns* HEATHCLIFF *to mirror above fireplace)* Now look here in the glass—see those lines between your eyebrows and those black eyes—like fiends?

HEATHCLIFF. Yes.

ELLEN. Well, smooth out those wrinkles.

HEATHCLIFF. *(Turning back to* ELLEN*)* You want me to wish for a smooth forehead and blue eyes like Linton. I do—so long as that's what Cathy admires.

ELLEN. A good heart will help you to a handsome face, my boy.

HEATHCLIFF. Don't cant, Nell.

ELLEN. *(As the comb snags in his tangled hair)*

Goodness! When did you comb it last? Now, that's better—it's out of your eyes at least. *(Standing him in front of the mirror)* Tell me, don't you think yourself rather handsome?

HEATHCLIFF. *(Straightening collar)* Yes—maybe—

ELLEN. I tell you I do. You're fit for a prince in disguise.

HEATHCLIFF. *(With contempt)* A prince!

ELLEN. Why not? Who knows but your father was Emperor of Persia and your mother an Indian Queen—each of them able to buy up Wuthering Heights and the Grange on a week's income?

HEATHCLIFF. *(Turning back)* That's silly.

ELLEN. Not at all. I'm certain you were kidnapped and brought to England by wicked sailors. Stand straight. Oh, it's a pity you can't remember any of that language Joseph talks about.

HEATHCLIFF. Well, I can't. I think I remember something about boats and the sea, but it may be only a dream I remember. All I really know is the moor and Wuthering, and, of course, Cathy.

ELLEN. Just the same, if I were you I'd claim high birth.

HEATHCLIFF. *(Laughing)* Like Linton!

ELLEN. *(Crossing up to door Right with wash basin)* Linton. Don't talk to me about Linton! High birth! A squire—pooh! What's a squire? (ELLEN *throws water out the door.)*

CATHERINE. *(Upstairs)* What time is it, Nelly?

ELLEN. It's nearly eight. *(To* HEATHCLIFF*)* Now stand there so Cathy'll see you.

(HEATHCLIFF *steps forward.)*

CATHERINE. *(Descending stairs)* Oh, *why* doesn't Edgar come! (CATHERINE *passes* HEATHCLIFF *without noticing him and runs to the window. Not seeing her guest approaching, she turns away, annoyed)* The devil! Nell, am I all right?

ELLEN. You *look* very nice.

HEATHCLIFF. You're beautiful.

CATHERINE. *(As though she had not seen him before)* Oh! *(To* ELLEN*)* Clasp my necklace, please— I can't manage it. *(Crosses Left to settle.)*

ELLEN. You're being very grand tonight, aren't you?

CATHERINE. *(Handing* ELLEN *the necklace)* Ellen! (CATHERINE *sits down carefully)* Mind my curls.

ELLEN. *(Behind settle)* You should be sending to London for a lady's maid.

CATHERINE. Perhaps I shall go to London and fetch one myself.

ELLEN. And I suppose you'll have tea at the palace.

CATHERINE. Maybe.

(ELLEN *fusses with* CATHERINE'S *hair; and* HEATHCLIFF *sits on floor before her, his face shining.)*

ELLEN. You may notice Heathcliff's been donning himself.

CATHERINE. Donning! Nell, will you never stop using such vulgar expressions?

HEATHCLIFF. *(Smoothing his hair)* Nelly did it.

CATHERINE. I should think you were old enough to wash yourself.

HEATHCLIFF. I'm going to do a lot of washing from now on.

CATHERINE. So I trust.

HEATHCLIFF. *(Annoyed)* You've only just taken to washing yourself.

CATHERINE. *(Hotly)* That's a lie! I've always washed, haven't I, Nell?

ELLEN. Only on Sundays. You were a very dirty child—dirtier than Heathcliff, if possible.

CATHERINE. *(Crushingly)* Ellen!

(There is a silence.)

HEATHCLIFF. Cathy—would you do something for me?

CATHERINE. That depends.

HEATHCLIFF. *(Seriously)* It's unreasonable, I know—but—

CATHERINE. If it's unreasonable, don't ask. Oh, Nell, you've mussed my hair. That's enough. Let me alone. (ELLEN *sighs, and goes into kitchen.)* Well, Heathcliff, what is it?

HEATHCLIFF. *(Sullen)* Nothing.

CATHERINE. There—I didn't mean to be sharp. *(He is glowering at the floor. Impulsively* CATHER-INE *makes a move to sit beside him. Remembering her dress, however, she takes a pillow, places it on the floor and sits carefully, arranging her dress. She watches* HEATHCLIFF *for an instant, then takes his hand and speaks tenderly)* Heathcliff— (HEATH-CLIFF *looks up at her and smiles. She laughs)* Dearest, sullen Heathcliff—

HEATHCLIFF. *(Suddenly, after a pause)* Don't turn me out for him.

CATHERINE. *(Withdrawing her hand)* Is that what you wanted to ask?

HEATHCLIFF. Yes. *(After a silence, encouraged, he continues)* When Linton comes, have Ellen say you're out.

CATHERINE. I'll not.

HEATHCLIFF. *(An instant's pause)* I never see you—

CATHERINE. Never see me, indeed! You see me every day.

HEATHCLIFF. I know—but it isn't the same—

CATHERINE. Of course it isn't. We're no longer children. We can't spend our lives running together on the moors.

HEATHCLIFF. *(Seriously)* I know.

CATHERINE. *(Very ladylike)* Oh, it was very nice to go barefoot and dirty, to be free as the air, racing and laughing on the heath all day—but now, Heathcliff, I'm a young lady, and you—you have work to do.

HEATHCLIFF. *(Surprised)* I've always had work to do.

CATHERINE. And I suppose you're angry because I don't help you any more?

HEATHCLIFF. No.

CATHERINE. I must think of my hands—Isabel has lovely hands.

HEATHCLIFF. Damn Isabel!

CATHERINE. Of course I don't want to be like her—but that's no reason why I shouldn't wish for pretty hands.

HEATHCLIFF. I think they're pretty.

CATHERINE. You know nothing about such matters. I want to have soft hands and pretty dresses, and I want to live in a beautiful house like the Grange.

HEATHCLIFF. Like the Grange—

CATHERINE. Oh, Heathcliff, you can't believe how splendid it is—carpets everywhere, high white ceilings, and showers of crystal drops!

HEATHCLIFF. I wouldn't exchange Wuthering for the Grange, no matter how many carpets and crystal lamps.

CATHERINE. *(Lightly)* Not even if I were living there—and commanded you to—?

HEATHCLIFF. If you were living there—?

CATHERINE. *(Noticing his troubled look)* I was only teasing, Heathcliff—

HEATHCLIFF. I'd not exchange Wuthering for the

Grange, even though you let me toss Joseph from the highest gable and painted the housefront with Hindley's blood.

ELLEN. *(Re-enters with a tray for* HINDLEY*)* Toss Joseph from the highest—! Well, I declare!

CATHERINE. *(Laughing)* Oh, Ellen, don't pretend to be so shocked.

ELLEN. As rude as savages—both of you. *(Exits upstairs with tray.)*

CATHERINE. Heathcliff, when Edgar goes I'll slip out of this dress and we'll climb the crag. The moon's high tonight, and we'll be able to see the whole valley from Thrushcross to Kendal. Would that please you, Heathcliff?

HEATHCLIFF. *(Uncertainly)* Yes, Cathy, but—

CATHERINE. Why are you unhappy, Heathcliff? I said we'd walk together after Edgar goes.

HEATHCLIFF. Yes—after Edgar—

CATHERINE. Very well—if you're going to be disagreeable—

HEATHCLIFF. *(Catching her hand)* Only look at the almanac! *(He points to calendar which hangs on the wall)* The crosses are for the evenings you've spent with Linton and the dots for those you've spent with me. I've marked every day.

CATHERINE. Yes, very foolish—as if I took notice. And where's the sense of it?

HEATHCLIFF. To show you that I *do* take notice.

CATHERINE. *(Irritated)* And why should I always be sitting with you? What good do I get? What do you talk about? You might as well be dumb or a baby for anything you say to amuse me—or for anything you do, either!

HEATHCLIFF. You never told me before that I talked too little or that you disliked my company.

CATHERINE. It's no company at all when people know nothing and say nothing! (HEATHCLIFF *goes over to the fireplace and stands with his back to* CATHERINE. *She is about to speak, but does not. There is a KNOCK at door Right.)* Oh, that must be Edgar! (CATHERINE *jumps up, touching her hair and dress)* Answer the door, Ellen.

(ELLEN *re-enters; goes out Right.)*

EDGAR. *(Off Right. Politely)* Good evening, Mrs. Dean. How are you?
ELLEN. I'm quite well, thank you. Come in.

(EDGAR LINTON *enters. He is an exceedingly handsome young man, slender, fair and immaculately dressed.)*

CATHERINE. *(Running to him)* Edgar!
EDGAR. *(Center. Taking her hands)* Catherine dearest! I'm not too early, I hope.
CATHERINE. No, not too early—never too early—

(EDGAR *catches sight of* HEATHCLIFF. *There is an awkward silence.)*

EDGAR. *(Coldly)* Good evening, Heathcliff.
HEATHCLIFF. *(Savagely)* You don't have to speak to me.
CATHERINE. How dare you talk like that! Apologize to Edgar at once.

(HEATHCLIFF *stares at* EDGAR, *laughs rudely and goes out Right.* CATHERINE, *furious, crosses to door and calls after him. There is no reply.)*

EDGAR. *(Breaking Left above settle)* Your friend has nice manners. *(A pause)* A good beating wouldn't hurt him.
CATHERINE. *(Turning on him)* Well, suppose you give him one!

EDGAR. I wasn't really criticizing, only—

CATHERINE. *(Crossing Center)* Oh, yes, you were, and you needn't. After all, Heathcliff hasn't had your advantages. He says what he thinks and you don't—which doesn't mean your thoughts are better! *(Turns away Right.)*

EDGAR. Now, Catherine—please—

CATHERINE. *(To* ELLEN, *who is fussing about, dusting)* Well, Ellen—?

ELLEN. Yes.

CATHERINE. *(Sharply)* What are you doing?

ELLEN. My work, Miss.

CATHERINE. You have no work to do now.

ELLEN. I'm sure Mr. Linton will excuse me.

CATHERINE. *(Going to her)* Take yourself and your rags off.

ELLEN. I'm sorry for it, but I shall stay. It's my duty.

CATHERINE. *(Snatching dust rag)* We want no spying.

ELLEN. I'm not spying. A young lady must have a chaperone—your father would have wished it.

CATHERINE. Leave the room, Ellen.

ELLEN. No. (CATHERINE *pinches her.)* Oh, Miss, that's a nasty trick! You've no right to nip me, and I'll not bear it.

CATHERINE. I didn't touch you.

ELLEN. *(Showing arm)* What's that, then?

EDGAR. *(Crossing to* CATHERINE*)* Catherine, love, Catherine!

CATHERINE. Leave the room, Ellen. *(Pushes* EL-LEN.*)*

EDGAR. *(Stopping her)* Catherine, you mustn't—

CATHERINE. What right have you to interfere?

(A tense pause, then CATHERINE *slaps him. A silence.* EDGAR *crosses to door Right.)*

ELLEN. It's a kindness, sir, to let you know her true nature.

CATHERINE. Where are you going? *(She runs to him)* No, you mustn't go.

EDGAR. *(Coldly)* I must.

CATHERINE. No, not yet. Sit down. You shan't leave me in a temper. I'd be miserable all night—and I won't be miserable for *you.*

EDGAR. Can I stay after you've struck me? *(Pause)* You make me ashamed of you. I'll not come here again. *(A silence.* CATHERINE *seems about to cry.)* And you told a deliberate untruth.

CATHERINE. *(Crossing over Left)* I did nothing deliberately. Well, go if you please! Get away! Oh, dear—I want to die— *(Sinks upon the settle.)*

ELLEN. *(Going toward kitchen)* Miss is dreadfully wayward, sir. You'd better be riding home, else she'll be sick—if only to grieve us.

EDGAR. *(Undecided)* But I can't leave her like this—

ELLEN. You'll be wiser if you do. A good cry won't hurt her. (ELLEN *goes out to kitchen.)*

EDGAR. *(Pauses a moment, then crosses and touches* CATHERINE'S *shoulder)* Catherine.

CATHERINE. *(Rising and clinging to him)* Oh, Edgar— *(Suddenly, by an irresistible impulse, they embrace passionately.* CATHERINE *sinks on settle.* EDGAR, *shaken a little, stands by awkwardly.* CATHERINE, *after a silence)* Sit down, Edgar. You look so foolish standing there!

EDGAR. *(Sitting beside her)* Then you do—forgive me?

CATHERINE. For what?

EDGAR. For—well—

CATHERINE. Don't be a fool.

EDGAR. I don't like to hear you talk that way, Cathy.

CATHERINE. But you are being a fool. Why should you be ashamed because you kissed me?

EDGAR. I only want you to know that I do respect you.

CATHERINE. I'd rather you loved me. I respect no one, and I ask no one to respect me.

EDGAR. You have the most extraordinary ideas, Cathy.

CATHERINE. They seem very natural to me.

EDGAR. But, dearest, haven't you any sense for— the ordinary decencies—?

CATHERINE. Now, Edgar, don't! If you lecture me you'll spoil everything.

EDGAR. I only wanted to say—

CATHERINE. *(Turning front. Interrupting)* How is Isabel?

EDGAR. *(A trifle coldly)* She's very well, except for a slight summer cold, and she sends you her love.

CATHERINE. *(Also coldly)* And you may take her mine.

EDGAR. *(After a pause)* We both find it lonely at the Grange.

CATHERINE. I'm sorry.

EDGAR. Don't you find it lonely here since your father's—death?

CATHERINE. No—there's Heathcliff. Of course, since Father died, Hindley's been very hard on Heathcliff. Sometimes I almost wish he were dead too.

EDGAR. What a shocking thing to say, Catherine!

CATHERINE. You wouldn't want me to lie, would you?

EDGAR. You needn't lie, but you don't have to say it— Besides, it's hard to understand what you see in Heathcliff.

CATHERINE. Let's not talk about Heathcliff.

EDGAR. He's certainly common—

CATHERINE. *(Hotly)* Then don't talk about him. *(A pause.)*

EDGAR. Catherine, please tell me something—and don't be angry.

CATHERINE. What is it?

EDGAR. It's about Heathcliff.

CATHERINE. Oh, Edgar, we shall quarrel.

EDGAR. Please, dear, I only want to know— Has he ever— *(Ashamed)* Has he ever done—what I did tonight?

CATHERINE. *(Surprised)* Oh, you mean has he ever kissed me—as you did? *(Laughs contemptuously)* No, Heathcliff and I don't kiss.

EDGAR. But you have kissed—you don't deny it!

CATHERINE. *(Rising and crossing Center)* No, I don't. You remember the time I had the fever and you weren't allowed to see me? Well, Heathcliff kissed me then. He wanted to catch it too, but he didn't. And once after Joseph gave him an awful beating I kissed him—a lot of times. But it wasn't at all like us—it was quite different.

EDGAR. Then you don't really care for him.

CATHERINE. But I do.

EDGAR. Though not in the way you do for me.

CATHERINE. No—not in the same way.

EDGAR. *(Rising and crossing to her)* Oh, Cathy, I'm glad! *(A pause)* You will marry me, won't you? You must know how deeply I love you. *(A pause)* Cathy, will you be my wife?

CATHERINE. *(After a pause, quietly)* Yes.

EDGAR. *(After a pause)* Aren't you glad—haven't you anything else to say?

CATHERINE. No.

EDGAR. But you are glad!

CATHERINE. *(Irritated)* Of course I'm glad—but don't make me *say* it. *(Sweetly, holding out her arms to him)* Edgar—

(EDGAR *kisses her gently on the lips, and* CATHER-
INE *throws her arms about him happily. There
is a roll of distant THUNDER.* EDGAR *pulls
himself away and listens.)*

EDGAR. What was that?

CATHERINE. I heard nothing.

EDGAR. There's going to be a storm. I'm sure I
heard thunder.

CATHERINE. *(Delighted)* Oh, I love storms—
they're wonderful here on the heights!

EDGAR. *(Pleasantly, but a trifle hurt)* Remember,
dear, I've a three mile ride on the open moor.

CATHERINE. *(Running to window Right)* Damn
your ride!

EDGAR. Catherine!

CATHERINE. What a lovely night! There—a flash!
We're going to have a real storm!

EDGAR. I'm afraid I don't find it so amusing. If
I'm to make the Grange, dear, I must start at once.

CATHERINE. No—don't go. Not tonight! Edgar,
please— I know—you must stay here. That's it—
you shall spend the night and go home in the morning.

EDGAR. Catherine! In the first place, Isabel would
be terribly worried—and what would the servants
think?

CATHERINE. Oh, forget them all—just once! Stay
with me—we'll watch the storm together.

EDGAR. *(In a fatherly tone)* You are an impulsive
child.

CATHERINE. You talk like an old man—and sometimes you act like one.

EDGAR. Aren't you being unreasonable, Catherine?
After all, there are others to be considered.

CATHERINE. Isabel wouldn't *die.* You're being
stupid.

EDGAR. *(Hurt)* You may call it that.

CATHERINE. Oh, Edgar, I'm sorry. I just don't want you to go—not tonight— *(Hopefully)* Maybe there won't be a storm. *(Distant THUNDER.)*

EDGAR. But I'll come again tomorrow—

CATHERINE. Well, you needn't come ever—it won't matter to me.

EDGAR. *(Taking her hand)* Love, you don't mean that—

CATHERINE. No, I don't mean it— Only I've looked forward to being with you all evening. Nelly has made cakes— Oh, dear—

EDGAR. But you do understand, don't you?

CATHERINE. Yes—I understand. *(A sound of faint THUNDER. ELLEN enters carrying a tray of food.)* Edgar is going, Ellen.

ELLEN. But I've fixed a nice supper—

CATHERINE. *(Sharply)* He's got to get back to the Grange before the storm breaks, hasn't he?

EDGAR. I'm sorry, Mrs. Dean, Isabel would be worried.

ELLEN. Of course. Is your horse in the stable?

EDGAR. *(Crossing up toward Right door)* No. I tethered her by the door.

CATHERINE. *(Following. Hopefully)* You might wait until after—

EDGAR. It may last for hours—and the roads would be drenched.

CATHERINE. *(With a note of sarcasm)* Should I ask Heathcliff to go along with you? He doesn't mind rain.

EDGAR. *(Ignoring this)* Good night, Catherine.

CATHERINE. *(Crosses front of EDGAR to door)* I'll come as far as the gate with you.

EDGAR. Good night, Mrs. Dean.

ELLEN. Good night, Master Linton. It's a pity you must go just when supper's ready.

EDGAR. I'm sorry too, Mrs. Dean. Good night.

(CATHERINE *and* EDGAR *go out Right, hand in hand. The THUNDER is repeated.* HEATHCLIFF *re-enters from the kitchen.)*

HEATHCLIFF. Has he gone?

ELLEN. Yes—on account of the storm.

HEATHCLIFF. What storm? *(Laughs.)*

ELLEN. Now say nothing to put her in a temper.

HEATHCLIFF. *(Moving to fireplace)* Ha! I'll say nothing— It's a good joke, though.

(CATHERINE *enters. A silence falls.)*

CATHERINE. What are you smirking at?

HEATHCLIFF. I'm not smirking.

CATHERINE. *(Moving Center)* You are! You may sneer if you wish, but Edgar had to go home for his sister's sake. (HEATHCLIFF *smiles.)* He has some consideration for others—which is more than can be said of you. *(A pause. She goes on explaining)* I asked him to stay all night, but he wouldn't for fear of worrying Isabel. I think that was very considerate, don't you, Ellen?

ELLEN. Oh, yes.

HEATHCLIFF. Considerate of Isabel, perhaps.

CATHERINE. What do you mean?

ELLEN. Now, Heathcliff—

HEATHCLIFF. *(Laughing)* You spend all day getting ready for him, and he stays a bare half hour.

CATHERINE. Can I help the weather?

HEATHCLIFF. You didn't make him forget it.

CATHERINE. I suppose you mean he doesn't care for me!

HEATHCLIFF. Not enough to get wet.

CATHERINE. *(Furious)* One would expect such a

remark from you. What Edgar said of you was right.

HEATHCLIFF. *(Hotly)* What did he say?

ELLEN. Both of you—stop!

CATHERINE. He said you were common—and I agreed with him—I agreed. *(A ghastly pause)* And as to caring for me—he asked me to marry him. That should prove he cares for me.

HEATHCLIFF. *(Stunned)* Marry him—

CATHERINE. Yes!

HEATHCLIFF. Cathy—you didn't—

CATHERINE. Didn't what?

HEATHCLIFF. Accept him.

CATHERINE. I did! I did!

HEATHCLIFF. *(Grasping her shoulders)* You can't do it! I'll never let you go—not to him! Cathy, you don't mean what you're saying.

CATHERINE. *(Freeing self)* Take your hands off me! I do mean it. Why shouldn't I marry Edgar? He loves me. Whom else should I marry? Do you think I'd marry you?

HEATHCLIFF. *(After a pause, softly)* No.

CATHERINE. And you're right. I wouldn't marry you and I'll tell you why— I wouldn't marry you because you'd degrade me—degrade me—do you understand? *(A dreadful silence falls. HEATHCLIFF stares at CATHERINE, his face tortured. Suddenly he rushes out Right. The THUNDER is heard again, nearer this time. Sinking down on settle—with childish misery)* Oh, I'm very unhappy—

ELLEN. *(About to take out food)* A pity.

CATHERINE. *(Sweetly)* No, Ellen, darling, let's eat it ourselves. I'll call Heathcliff back and we'll have a party all our own. I didn't mean to make him angry.

ELLEN. Make him angry! Well, I must say—

CATHERINE. *(At door Right)* Heathcliff! *(There is no reply. A pause—surprised)* He won't answer.

ELLEN. Small wonder!

CATHERINE. But where do you suppose he is?

ELLEN. Probably in the loft, sulking.

CATHERINE. It's cruel of him.

ELLEN. Cruel—to be sure!

CATHERINE. *(Crosses down Right—sits bench)* Well, let him sulk, then— I hope he's as miserable as I.

ELLEN. You're hard to please. So many friends and so few cares, and you can't be happy.

CATHERINE. Now don't *you* be angry with me. Sit here by me—please. Oh, Nell, I'm so worried. *(A pause)* It's about Edgar. Tell me—should I have done it?

ELLEN. Done what?

CATHERINE. Promised to marry him, of course.

ELLEN. Why should we discuss it? You've given your word.

CATHERINE. But say whether I should have done so.

ELLEN. Very well. Do you love Mr. Edgar?

CATHERINE. Of course I do.

ELLEN. And *why* do you love him?

CATHERINE. Nonsense—I do. That's sufficient.

ELLEN. By no means. Tell me why.

CATHERINE. Well, because he's handsome.

ELLEN. Bad.

CATHERINE. And because he loves me.

ELLEN. Indifferent.

CATHERINE. *(Rising and crossing Center)* Then he's rich—and I'll be the greatest lady in the County. And I shall be proud of having such a husband.

ELLEN. Then that settles it. Marry Mr. Linton.

CATHERINE. *(Returning to settle)* I don't want your permission for that. I *shall* marry him—but you haven't told me whether I'm right.

ELLEN. *(Sits bench)* Perfectly right—if people

are right to marry only for the present. You'll escape a rough home for a wealthy one— Where's the obstacle?

CATHERINE. *(Striking her breast)* Here! In my heart I'm convinced I am wrong.

ELLEN. Strange—

CATHERINE. *(Sinks to the floor and rests on* ELLEN'S *knees. A pause)* Ellen, I've dreamt dreams that have stayed with me ever after and changed my ideas—they've gone through me like wine through water.

ELLEN. *(Hastily)* Oh, Cathy, don't! We're dismal enough.

CATHERINE. *(Catching her hands)* You must listen— *(THUNDER.* ELLEN *rises. Holding her.)* Stay, Ellen— I only wanted to say that if I were in Heaven I should be wretched.

ELLEN. Because you're not fit to go there.

CATHERINE. It's not for that. I dreamt once that I was there. I was there, but Heaven didn't seem to be my home. I broke my heart with weeping to come back to earth, and the angels were so angry that they flung me out into the middle of the heath, near Wuthering, and I awoke sobbing for joy. *(A pause)* I've no more right to marry Edgar than to be in Heaven; and if Hindley and Joseph hadn't brought Heathcliff so low, I wouldn't think of it.

ELLEN. Then it's Heathcliff you love—

CATHERINE. I don't know— He isn't handsome, and sometimes I hate him. But I know this—he's more myself than I am. Whatever we're made of, he and I are the same—and Linton's as different as frost from fire.

ELLEN. And as soon as you become Mrs. Linton, Heathcliff loses friend, love and all— *(As though to herself)* I wonder how he'll bear the separation?

CATHERINE. Separation! What's to separate us? Nelly, you'll think me selfish, but if Heathcliff and

I married, we should be beggars—while if I marry Linton I can aid Heathcliff to rise.

ELLEN. *(Firmly)* I think that's the worst reason you've given for marrying Mr. Linton.

CATHERINE. It's not! It's the best. The others were to satisfy my whims, and for Edgar's sake to please him. Don't you see that if I lost Heathcliff the world would turn into a stranger. I should not even be a part of it. Oh, Ellen, I *am* Heathcliff. He's always in my mind—not as a pleasure any more than I am a pleasure to myself, but as my own being. So don't talk of separation again. It's impossible and— *(Heavy THUNDER.)* Oh, where is he? Why doesn't he come in! *(Goes to door Right; calls)* Heathcliff— Heathcliff— Nelly, I've been cruel to him tonight. I must find him—

ELLEN. *(Crossing after* CATHERINE) Cathy—the storm's breaking—you're not going out.

CATHERINE. I am—let me go! Heathcliff! *(Runs out Right, calling.)*

HINDLEY. *(Reappears on the stairs)* In God's name, what's the matter?

ELLEN. Heathcliff won't come in, and Catherine must go after him. *(Calls)* Catherine!

(JOSEPH re-enters from Right.)

HINDLEY. *(Drunkenly)* The devil take her!

JOSEPH. *(With grim relish—moving toward kitchen)* After the lads as usual! A fine 'ne runnin' after a dog of a gypsy—but tonight she'll not find him—not tonight. I'd never wonder he's at the bottom of a bog hole.

ELLEN. What do you mean? Have you seen Heathcliff? *(JOSEPH disappears into the kitchen without replying. ELLEN is about to follow him, but instead calls:)* Catherine, come in—come in!

(After an instant CATHERINE *re-enters. From this point until the end of the Act the STORM continues furiously.)*

CATHERINE. *(Wildly)* He doesn't answer—and the gate's open!

ELLEN. The wind blew it open.

CATHERINE. No—no, I latched it myself when I let Edgar out.   *(WARN Curtain.)*

HINDLEY. Stop that yelling and get upstairs.

CATHERINE. *(At foot of stairs)* I wonder where he is! I wonder where—

HINDLEY. *(Seizing* CATHERINE'S *arm)* Did you hear what I said!?

CATHERINE. *(Freeing herself)* Take your hands off me, you drunken fool! What did I say, Nelly? I've forgotten. *(Crossing down Right)* Was he vexed by my bad humor tonight? Dear, tell me what I've said to hurt him? Oh, I do wish he'd come in.

JOSEPH. *(Re-enters, an open Bible in his hands. Reading)* "And I will lay thy flesh upon the mountains—"

CATHERINE. *(A step toward* JOSEPH*)* Have you seen Heathcliff?

JOSEPH. *(Continuing)* "I will also water with thy blood the land."

CATHERINE. *(Screaming)* Have you seen Heathcliff, you fool!

JOSEPH. *(With satisfaction)* Yes—I seed him.

CATHERINE. Where—where!

JOSEPH. *(Vividly)* He rand past me, his face torn like one that's dying, and he ran down the road and into the dark. The devil's gone back to his kind, and we'll see him no more!

CATHERINE. *(Hysterically)* No—no! Heathcliff! *(Runs out Right, calling.)*

ELLEN. Catherine! Come back! You'll catch your death— Catherine! *(Follows* CATHERINE *out.)*

HINDLEY. *(Closing door behind them)* We'll see him no more—

JOSEPH. *(With quiet exhaltation)* "And all the bright lights of Heaven will I make dark above thee, and set darkness upon thy land—"

CURTAIN

ACT TWO

Scene I

The Scene: *The drawing room at Threscomb Grange. An afternoon in early autumn, several years later.*
A lofty Georgian room, richly and beautifully furnished. The prevailing colors are red and cream. Large French windows at Right; door to hall rear Right Center; door to pantry rear Left Center; door down Left. Fireplace and bookcases Left. Table and two chairs at window down Right; chair up Right; table Center at back; sofa at fire with table behind it; armchair below fire; tea table and chairs Center.

At Rise: Ellen *is fussing about the tea table.* Isabel, *a commonplace though pretty girl, is standing at the French windows looking out. She holds a book marked by her index finger. The afternoon light is beginning to fail.*

Isabel. *(Romantically)* Wuthering Heights! How dark it looms against the sky tonight!
Ellen. *(Arranging table—very practical)* Milk, bread and jam.
Isabel. There's nothing in all the countryside to compare with Wuthering.
Ellen. Must you always go on about Wuthering?
Isabel. *(A trifle indignant)* Go on about Wuthering! I like that!

40

ELLEN. Knives—spoons—napkins—

ISABEL. Go on about Wuthering! Why, Edgar doesn't even allow me to mention Wuthering.

ELLEN. Then why do you?

ISABEL. *(Crossing a step toward* ELLEN*)* Are you implying, Ellen, that I disobey my brother?

ELLEN. Oh, no.

ISABEL. *(Primly)* Of course, I never mention it to Catherine because I love her and I wouldn't want to—to agitate her, but, after all, there's no reason we shouldn't talk about it.

ELLEN. And there's no reason why we should.

ISABEL. *(Winningly)* Come, Ellen—tell me about Wuthering—please—

ELLEN. There's nothing to tell—you know that. It's lonely and cold and many people have died there. It's like all old houses, and there's an end.

ISABEL. But, since Hindley drank himself to death, there are so many stories about Wuthering. People say— (ISABEL *is interrupted by* CATHERINE, *who enters Right Center, crosses down Left and sits by the fireplace; begins to sew.* CATHERINE *is somewhat matured and considerably subdued.* ELLEN *goes out Left Center.* ISABEL *sits down Right, opens her book and pretends to read. She looks at* CATHERINE *once or twice before she speaks)* Catherine, dear, this is the most harrowing book.

CATHERINE. Is it?

ISABEL. Don't you dote on Mrs. Radcliffe?

CATHERINE. *(Indifferently)* Who is Mrs. Radcliffe?

ISABEL. Who is she! She's the author of this book—"The Mysteries of Udolpho." And she also wrote "The Orphan of the Castle." I love her novels. They're so terrifying and genteel.

CATHERINE. I'm afraid I shall never care about reading.

ISABEL. But you must read "The Mysteries of Udolpho!" It all takes place in a haunted castle, and there is a beautiful dark hero and a great many ghosts who wander about after sunset. I love the heroine too. She's not in very good health and her aunt's enemies are plotting to kill her. I know they will be foiled, however.

CATHERINE. How do you know?

ISABEL. I read the ending, but even if I hadn't I should have known. In Mrs. Radcliffe's novels the good never die.

CATHERINE. *(Bored)* If I wrote a novel I should have all the bad people kill all the good people.

ISABEL. *(Shocked)* Catherine! That wouldn't be nice.

CATHERINE. It might.

ISABEL. *(Firmly)* It would be horrible—horrible and unjust. Don't you believe that good people always triumph?

CATHERINE. Yes. I believe that's what makes them so certain they're good. I'd like to fool them, you see.

ISABEL. You can't mean that.

CATHERINE. Oh, I really don't care— *(A pause.)*

ISABEL. *(Rising. Primly)* Just the same, you should read "The Mysteries of Udolpho."

CATHERINE. But I don't want to.

ISABEL. I thought you might—because the castle is so much like— *(A pause)* Wuthering Heights.

CATHERINE. *(Startled)* Like Wuthering!

ISABEL. Yes.

CATHERINE. Wuthering isn't haunted.

ISABEL. Some say it is.

CATHERINE. Don't let's talk of Wuthering.

ISABEL. But why—?

CATHERINE. Because I've been trying to forget it—for so long.

ISABEL. *(Crossing Center)* If you really hate Wuthering, why don't you sell it?

CATHERINE. I don't hate it— I—

ISABEL. Certainly you never go there. You haven't been there since your brother's death.

CATHERINE. No—I haven't— *(A pause.)*

ISABEL. *(Crossing toward* CATHERINE*)* Oh, Catherine, dearest, let's go up to Wuthering sometime and explore. There *are* secret panels, aren't there?

CATHERINE. Don't be absurd.

ISABEL. *(Breaking up to above tea table. Shuddering)* There should be. I almost feel inspired to write a novel about it. Joseph would be the phantom of the place, and I should have the heroine discover a mangled corpse in that grove of firs behind the house.

CATHERINE. You've been reading too many novels.

ISABEL. But Wuthering *is* mysterious. All the people in Gimmerton are afraid of it. They say it's full of ghosts. *(A pause. A step toward* CATHERINE*)* They even say Heathcliff's spirit walks there.

CATHERINE. *(Rises)* Heathcliff isn't dead.

ISABEL. You've never heard from him—not a word. How can you know?

CATHERINE. *(Crossing Center)* I know, I tell you, I *know!* That's enough.

ISABEL. Of course, I don't believe what people say because I know that ghosts don't really exist. *(Moving up behind* CATHERINE*)* Just the same, Joseph swears that windy nights Heathcliff beats on the shutters and calls to be let in—

CATHERINE. *(Wildly)* Don't! Don't talk like that! I'll not let you say such things! They're lies and I won't believe them!

ISABEL. *(Innocently)* Why, Catherine—!

CATHERINE. Heathcliff isn't dead, I tell you.

(CATHERINE'S *voice suddenly takes a strange note of fear*) Ellen! Ellen! Ellen—where are you? (EL-LEN *enters Left Center hurriedly.* CATHERINE *clasps her hand tightly*) Oh, Ellen, there you are—

ELLEN. What is it, Cathy? Is something wrong?

CATHERINE. No, nothing, only—

ELLEN. But you're trembling!

CATHERINE. *(Withdrawing her hand)* I'm all right. I was faint. *(Recovering herself)* I just wanted to tell you to light the candles.

ELLEN. Why, it's scarce four-thirty!

CATHERINE. It's dark, isn't it—and I hate the dark. *(A pause)* Where's Edgar?

ELLEN. Mr. Linton went down to Gimmerton. I believe he went to inquire about the new colt.

CATHERINE. As though I cared *why* he went! Serve tea when he returns.

ELLEN. *(Severely)* Catherine, you *are* trembling! What's the matter? Are you ill?

ISABEL. *(Putting arm around* CATHERINE*)* Catherine, dearest—

CATHERINE. Oh, don't talk to me—either of you! *(Leaves the room abruptly, Right Center.)*

ELLEN. Now what have you said to upset her?

ISABEL. *(Moving away Right. Innocently)* Nothing! I said nothing. We were merely talking about books and I happened to mention what people say about Wuthering being haunted and about Heathcliff's ghost calling.

ELLEN. You shouldn't have done that, Miss Linton.

ISABEL. *(Crossing to windows)* I know, but it's really your fault. If you'd been nice and talked with me about Wuthering, maybe I wouldn't have mentioned it to Catherine.

ELLEN. You should be ashamed of yourself, Isabel.

ISABEL. Well, I'm not. *(A pause)* Do you know,

Ellen, I sometimes believe Catherine longs to go back. On our walks she always looks toward the heights. She thinks I don't notice, but I do.

ELLEN. *(Above tea table. Firmly)* I'm sure Mrs. Linton is very happy here.

ISABEL. *(Breaking down to above chair Right. Seriously)* I'm not. Catherine is close. She never tells me what she thinks, but I can guess. I talked about Heathcliff today on purpose to see if she would be upset. Now I'm sure she hasn't forgotten.

ELLEN. Forgotten?

ISABEL. Him, of course. *(A pause—lightly)* They were very good friends, weren't they?

ELLEN. They were fond of each other—they grew up together.

ISABEL. I wonder if he's dead.

ELLEN. I can't see why that should interest you.

ISABEL. But it does. It was such a strange story—like a novel.

ELLEN. Catherine's fortunate to have a kind husband to take care of her, and you should be ashamed to torment her with memories your brother tried to make her forget. If he knew, he would be angry.

ISABEL. You won't tell—? (ELLEN *motions silence as* EDGAR *enters Right Center. He is obviously disturbed.)* Oh, Edgar, did you buy the colt?

EDGAR. *(Crossing to fireplace)* No, no—I didn't even see it.

ISABEL. I thought you went especially—

EDGAR. I did, but something rather disturbing has happened.

ISABEL. Happened! What?

EDGAR. *(After a pause)* Where's Catherine?

ISABEL. Upstairs. I'll go call her.

EDGAR. No—no, don't do that. As a matter of fact, I prefer not to have her here just now.

ISABEL. *(Crossing to* EDGAR*)* Edgar, what *has* happened?

EDGAR. *(A pause)* It's about Joseph—

ISABEL. How odd! We were just talking about him—Ellen and I were, that is.

EDGAR. He was found this morning wandering on the moor—mad.

ISABEL. It was living in that dreadful old house did it. Oh, I knew Wuthering was haunted.

ELLEN. Where is Joseph now?

EDGAR. At Holburn cottage. John found him covered with mud and half frozen. Doctor Kenneth says he must have been out the whole night.

ISABEL. How awful! Did you see him? What's he like?

EDGAR. He seemed to be quite helpless. He lay on the floor mumbling like an idiot, and when I tried to talk to him he cried out in fear, a cry that— *(He breaks off—turns away.)*

ISABEL. *(Shuddering)* Oh—

EDGAR. *(Without looking at ELLEN. With a certain tenseness)* You've seen no strangers about, have you, Ellen?

ELLEN. *(Down Right)* No, Mr. Linton, no one.

EDGAR. *(After a pause—turning to ELLEN)* Last night a strange light was seen at Wuthering.

ISABEL. A light! Who told you?

EDGAR. Tom Paine was returning late from Thornton, and when he passed below Wuthering he noticed a bright light burning between the shutters in the south wing. I questioned him particularly, and he insisted the light was in the upper southwest window. *(A pause)* Ellen, wasn't that Catherine's room?

ELLEN. Why, yes—yes, it was.

EDGAR. *(Crossing Center)* I thought so. It's doubtless nothing, but I can't help feeling uneasy. I tried to get some of the men to investigate, but not one of them would go near the place. They're a lot of miserable peasants with their fears and superstitions. Now they'll be sure Wuthering's haunted.

ISABEL. But it *is* exciting! If Joseph could only talk! Maybe it is haunted! Just this afternoon I was telling Catherine that Wuthering seems— *(Checks self.)*

EDGAR. *(Turning on her—his nerves on edge)* Haven't I asked you never to mention Wuthering Heights to Catherine?

ISABEL. But it wasn't I— You see, we were talking together and Ellen said—

EDGAR. I should think *you* would know better, Mrs. Dean.

ISABEL. *(Hurriedly)* It was really nothing. I'm sure Catherine wasn't even listening.

EDGAR. *(Controlling himself)* Neither is to mention what I have just told you. Do you understand, Ellen?

ELLEN. Yes, Mr. Linton. *I'll* say nothing.

EDGAR. Shall we have tea? It's late.

ELLEN. Yes, Mr. Linton. I'll serve tea directly. We were just waiting for you to come in.

EDGAR. Very well. We'll be down at once.

ISABEL. *(As they exit Right Center)* But, Edgar, did you ever hear of anything so mysterious! It gives me the strangest shivery feeling just to think of—

(ELLEN *goes out Left Center. The room is now in semi-darkness. A* FIGURE *appears outside the French window, opens it quietly and enters. It is* HEATHCLIFF. *He is plainly dressed and seems much older. He crosses up toward door Right Center, stops, turns back and glances about room. He moves down Left, pausing briefly above tea table. Hearing* ELLEN'S *steps, he quickly crosses down to below fireplace.* ELLEN *re-enters with a lighted taper; lights several candles. As she turns toward fireplace she catches sight of* HEATHCLIFF *standing in the shadow and utters a stifled cry.)*

HEATHCLIFF. *(Stepping forward)* No need to scream, Nell. You remember me.

ELLEN. You—! Heathcliff! Oh—

HEATHCLIFF. Yes.

ELLEN. *(Supporting herself against table)* I— Oh, seeing you there so—against the dark—it frightened me—

HEATHCLIFF. *(With a slight sneer)* Aren't you going to welcome me?

ELLEN. *(Getting control of herself—angrily)* How did you get in?

HEATHCLIFF. Aren't you glad to see me?

ELLEN. No—no, I'm not glad. Why did you come back?

HEATHCLIFF. *(Tensely)* Why did I come back! Why? You should know why.

ELLEN. You've got to go. Now—before they see you.

HEATHCLIFF. *(Taking her arm)* What are you talking about! You didn't used to be a fool, Nell.

ELLEN. Please, Heathcliff— You've no right to intrude here. She's happy with him.

HEATHCLIFF. *(Fiercely)* Happy with him! Is she? Tell me!

ELLEN. *(Weakly)* Yes.

HEATHCLIFF. You lie. She couldn't be happy—any more than I have been.

ELLEN. I always feared you'd come back—and now it's happened— *(Her voice breaking)* Oh, Heathcliff, leave them alone. If you stay only harm will come of it.

HEATHCLIFF. I'll harm no one—but I must see Catherine. I've got to. Take me to her, Ellen— I'm in Hell till you do!

ELLEN. I can't—not now. Mr. Linton's with her —and besides, I'd be afraid—

HEATHCLIFF. Afraid of Linton! *(Laughs.)*

ELLEN. No—afraid of the shock—the shock of seeing you—

HEATHCLIFF. Then she has missed me—?

ELLEN. I didn't say that. I was thinking of what happened—

HEATHCLIFF. Happened! What?

ELLEN. The night you left—she ran after you. I tried to call her back, but she wouldn't come—she wouldn't hear—she was like a wild thing.

HEATHCLIFF. *(Stunned)* She followed—me—?

ELLEN. Yes—and very nearly died for it. In the morning we found her, wet to the skin—burning with fever—crying for you. And she wouldn't stop crying—she was out of her head for days. Even people passing on the road could hear her, and sometimes I couldn't hold her down to the bed.

HEATHCLIFF. If only I'd known!

ELLEN. Now you know—so leave her alone. Go.

HEATHCLIFF. I'll never go.

ELLEN. You will if you care for Catherine. She's not well—she's never been well since that night. Doctor Kenneth says another attack of the fever would kill her.

HEATHCLIFF. Doctor Kenneth's a fool—and you're lying to me, Ellen. You've banded with Linton—I can see that. But you can't drive me away with lies. I'll see her, I tell you. Nothing can stop me! I'll—

ELLEN. Quiet—they'll hear you.

HEATHCLIFF. Let them.

ELLEN. No—no, please— Oh, Heathcliff, if you won't go, at least let me tell her—let me warn her. That's not much to ask, is it?

HEATHCLIFF. You'll tell her now—at once?

ELLEN. *(Crossing to door Left)* Yes—yes, I

promise—if only you'll come with me. They mustn't
find you here— Come!

(HEATHCLIFF *exits Left.* ELLEN *closes door behind
him. She quickly crosses to door Left Center.*
ISABEL *wanders in; goes to tea table; takes a
sandwich; sits on sofa.* ELLEN *exits. She returns almost immediately with tea things.*
CATHERINE *and* EDGAR *re-enter Right Center.*)

EDGAR. *(As they enter)* And, of course, the Vicar
sent his regards. He trusts to see you more often at
service. *(A pause)* He's an excellent man.

CATHERINE. *(Not listening)* Yes, excellent—and
so old too— *(Goes toward French windows.)*

EDGAR. I believe he is really fond of you, Catherine, and I know it grieves him that you do not take
a more active part in the Church work.

CATHERINE. *(Vaguely)* Do you think so?

EDGAR. *(Sits Right of tea table)* Why don't you
join one of the circles? It would occupy your time.

CATHERINE. *(At window)* How dark it is already!
Such short days, and summer nearly gone— *(A
pause)* I wonder if twilight isn't the darkest hour
of all—

ELLEN. *(Crossing to* CATHERINE. *Trying to get*
CATHERINE'S *attention)* Catherine, listen— I've
something I must tell you—

EDGAR. Come, come, Ellen, there's no sugar here.
It's rather absurd to forget the sugar. You might
as well forget the tea.

ELLEN. Oh, I'm sorry— I'll bring it directly. *(She
exits Left Center.)*

EDGAR. Don't you feel a draught, Isabel?
Catherine, is that window open?

CATHERINE. *(Startled)* What?

EDGAR. I asked if the window was open.

CATHERINE. Yes—a little.

EDGAR. Well, close it, please. (CATHERINE. *closes window.* ELLEN *re-enters with sugar.*) Ellen, that window was open.

ELLEN. *(Stammering)* Was it—?

EDGAR. Yes. And in the future I wish you'd be more careful. It doesn't matter about us, but I don't like to have Mrs. Linton sitting in a cold room. Catherine, aren't you coming to tea? (CATHERINE *sits Center tea table.* ISABEL *remains on sofa.* EDGAR *continues pleasantly)* It's been a beautiful day, hasn't it?

CATHERINE. Oh, Ellen, tarts—how nice!

EDGAR. Now, Catherine, please eat. You know what Doctor Kenneth says. *(Passes cakes.)*

CATHERINE. They look lovely— I'll try. *(Takes one)* You must have baked these yourself— Why, Nell, what is it? You look so—

ELLEN. Pardon me, ma'am, but there's someone— to see you.

CATHERINE. To see *me*—how odd!

EDGAR. Who is it?

ELLEN. *(Not looking at him)* A person, a man.

CATHERINE. What does he want?

ELLEN. I didn't question him.

EDGAR. Tell him to wait.

(A pause. ELLEN *is troubled.)*

CATHERINE. *(Her interest awakening)* Do I know him?

ELLEN. Yes—yes, you know him—but it's some-one you don't expect. *(A pause)* It's—

CATHERINE. *(Suddenly understanding)* Oh, Nell, it can't be! Is it—is it—?

(ELLEN *nods fearfully. With a little cry* CATHER-

INE *rises and quickly leaves the room Left Center.* ELLEN *follows.)*

EDGAR. Ellen, who is it? Ellen! Why do you suppose she didn't answer? I believe she left to avoid answering.

ISABEL. *(Rising)* Oh, I'm sure it's nothing. We're just nervous because of what happened at Wuthering. Why, it might even be the Vicar.

EDGAR. No, he told me he was having tea at home. You see, I particularly asked him to join us, and he wasn't able—

(CATHERINE *breaks into the room, too excited even to show joy.* ELLEN *appears in doorway.)*

CATHERINE. *(Crossing to* EDGAR*)* Oh, Edgar, Edgar, darling—

EDGAR. *(Rising. Annoyed)* What *is* it?

CATHERINE. Heathcliff! Heathcliff's come back!

EDGAR. You're joking!

CATHERINE. No, I mean it. It's true!

EDGAR. Well, there's no need to be absurd. After all, Heathcliff isn't the sort of person one—

CATHERINE. I know you don't like him, yet for my sake you must be friends. I'll tell him to come in. *(Starts to go Left.)*

EDGAR. *(Rising)* Catherine! Ellen, *you* tell him to come in. (ELLEN *goes out Left.)* And, Catherine, try to be glad without being absurd. The whole household need not see you welcome this runaway servant.

CATHERINE. You can't make me angry, Edgar, no matter what you say—not tonight, not tonight!

(HEATHCLIFF *enters Left. Calling his name,* CATHERINE *runs to him, seizes both his hands and draws him to where her husband is stand-*

ing. She places their hands together; they part almost at once. HEATHCLIFF *waits coolly for* EDGAR *to speak.)*

EDGAR. *(Stiffly)* Sit down, sir. Mrs. Linton would have me give you a cordial reception, and, of course, I am gratified when anything occurs to please her.

HEATHCLIFF. Thank you.

CATHERINE. You remember Isabel?

HEATHCLIFF. Yes, I remember her.

ISABEL. *(Above sofa. Confused and embarrassed)* And I remember you too. *(Laughs)* I used to see you at the Heights when—

CATHERINE. Tomorrow I shall think it a dream. I won't believe I've really seen you once more. And yet you don't deserve a welcome. To have been away and silent so long, and never to think of me—

HEATHCLIFF. I have thought of you, Cathy— You've never been out of my thoughts—

CATHERINE. Oh— *(A pause.)*

EDGAR. *(Testily)* Catherine, unless we are to have cold tea, please sit down. Your friend will have a long walk wherever he lodges tonight.

CATHERINE. Come, Heathcliff—here beside me. *(They sit,* HEATHCLIFF *Left of table;* CATHERINE *above table.* CATHERINE *serves. Gives* ISABEL *tea.* ISABEL *crosses down Right. Sits chair Right away from table)* I'm sure I shall spill it. *(Hands* EDGAR *a cup)* There, Edgar!

EDGAR. But you know I take milk.

CATHERINE. Then take it yourself, dear. *(*CATHERINE *forgets to serve.* EDGAR *eats nothing.)* Where have you been? Why didn't you write? How could you be so cruel?

HEATHCLIFF. Why should I have written?

CATHERINE. Did you know that I nearly died when you left me?

HEATHCLIFF. No. Ellen told me you'd been sick.
I didn't know of it before.

EDGAR. So it was Ellen who let you in.

HEATHCLIFF. No. I walked in myself—by that
door.

EDGAR. You mean you *walked* in without—without even—

CATHERINE. Of course that's what he means.
What difference how he got in? *(To* HEATHCLIFF*)*
I should be pleased had you smashed the front door.
How well you look! But you have changed! You've
grown older—much older. Where were you? You
disappeared into the night—completely. People
thought you were dead—said your spirit walked the
Heights. But I didn't believe them—I knew better.
Tell me—where were you? Where?

HEATHCLIFF. Everywhere.

CATHERINE. Where's everywhere?

HEATHCLIFF. I went to sea.

ISABEL. Oh, I've read all about the sea. It must
be beautiful.

HEATHCLIFF. Yes—beautiful—but lonely.

ISABEL. Were you ever in Africa? I've always
thought Africa must be one of the most interesting—

CATHERINE. *(Cutting her short)* Who cares about
Africa? Heathcliff—when did you return?

HEATHCLIFF. Only last night—late.

CATHERINE. But why didn't you come here?
Where did you stay?

HEATHCLIFF. At Wuthering Heights.

(ISABEL *utters a stifled cry.)*

EDGAR. You say you stayed at Wuthering?

HEATHCLIFF. Yes.

EDGAR. Did you see—was Joseph there?

HEATHCLIFF. Yes, he was there. Was surprised to see me, I think. *(Smiles.)*

EDGAR. *(Breathless)* You mean—?

HEATHCLIFF. I pounded on the shutter and called to be let in, and when he saw who it was he yelled like a madman and ran out of the house. I guess he thought he'd seen a ghost.

CATHERINE. *(Laughing)* A ghost! Oh, the fool would think that. He always said you'd gone back to Hell and the witches.

EDGAR. Catherine! Stop laughing.

CATHERINE. *(Gaily)* I can't—

EDGAR. Stop it, I say. Stop. You don't know what you're doing. You don't know that Joseph was found this morning—stark mad. *(Rises.)*

CATHERINE. Mad— (CATHERINE *stops laughing abruptly. A silence falls.* CATHERINE *and* HEATHCLIFF *stare at one another. A strange half smile creeps over his face.* CATHERINE *sees it; and suddenly she begins to laugh, this time with a touch of hysteria.)*

EDGAR. *(Alarmed)* Catherine! Catherine. What's the matter with you?

CATHERINE. It's like a judgment. We always hated Joseph—we used to plan how we should punish him. And now it's done—done without anyone lifting a hand.

EDGAR. You must realize, sir, that my wife is ill. Your coming has been most unfortunate, and I shall have to ask you to leave—at once.

ISABEL. Edgar!

HEATHCLIFF. Very well— I'll go. I only came to see Cathy.

CATHERINE. *(Blankly)* Where are you going?

HEATHCLIFF. To Wuthering Heights.

EDGAR. You can't stay there!

CATHERINE. Wuthering is as much his as mine.

It's *our* house. He may stay there as long as he wants—you've nothing to say about it.

EDGAR. *(Calming her)* Very well, Catherine—only be quiet. *(Sternly)* Heathcliff!

HEATHCLIFF. *(To* CATHERINE*)* I'll come again tomorrow. *(WARN Curtain.)*

CATHERINE. Yes—-tomorrow—without fail.

ISABEL. *(Hurriedly)* Oh, I'm so sorry, Mr.—Mr. Heathcliff.

EDGAR. *(Stiffly)* Goodnight.

HEATHCLIFF. Goodnight—Cathy.

ISABEL. *(Apologetically)* I'll come to the door with you— *(They go out Left.)*

(CATHERINE *rises from the table and moves about vacantly. Suddenly she throws herself on the sofa. She still smiles oddly.* EDGAR *watches her in alarm.)*

EDGAR. Catherine—are you all right?

CATHERINE. I, of course. Why do you ask?

(ISABEL *re-enters. She crosses directly to chair Right and speaks to* EDGAR. *She is facing the audience, however, her back to him.)*

ISABEL. Oh, Edgar—I was never so mortified.

EDGAR. *(Surprised)* Mortified!

ISABEL. How could you be so rude—asking him to leave! *(Covering her face)* Oh—

EDGAR. That common beggar!

ISABEL. Don't call him that! He's a gentleman. His loyalty to Catherine is beautiful—and I admire him. (ISABEL *sits.)*

(EDGAR *stares in blank amazement; and* CATHERINE *laughs again, softly, with a touch of mockery.)*

CURTAIN

ACT TWO

SCENE II

SCENE: *The same. A brilliant morning. Two weeks later.*

EDGAR *is opening a package of books at table Left, and* ELLEN *is on her knees, dusting a chair Right with considerable thoroughness. They work for a time in silence.*

ELLEN. Master Linton, we'll have to discharge Jenny.

EDGAR. *(Putting books in case; abstractedly)* Is she in trouble?

ELLEN. Goodness no. *(She rises)* But she leaves a trail of dust wherever she goes.

EDGAR. In that case I'll leave the dusting of these volumes to you. The bindings are very fine and I want them to be handled carefully.

ELLEN. Yes, Master Linton. *(She crosses to* EDGAR*)* My, they are lovely, aren't they?

EDGAR. Yes. *(Showing her a volume)* Binding by Bodoni.

ELLEN. *(Looking at volume, impressed)* Well! Hmmmm—poetry. *(Handing book back)* Yes, Master Linton, I'll dust them. I dare say they'll need it. *(*ELLEN *returns to her work and* EDGAR *places two or three more volumes in the bookcase.)*

EDGAR. *(Casually)* Oh, Ellen, do you know whether Mrs. Linton and Isabel are planning to walk with Heathcliff today?

ELLEN. Yes, sir, I'm afraid they are. Mrs. Linton asked to have a basket prepared. They're planning to lunch at Duxton Ridge.

EDGAR. *(Coldly)* That will be nice.

ELLEN. Yes, Master Linton.

EDGAR. By the way, how long were they out yesterday?

ELLEN. A little more than three hours.

EDGAR. *(Putting last books on chair)* I only asked because I'm a little worried about Catherine's health. So much exertion may not be good for her.

ELLEN. She is looking well, though.

EDGAR. *(Quietly)* Yes, she is. (EDGAR *crosses to French windows)* It's such a pleasant day—I think I'll take a little stroll myself.

ELLEN. *(Crossing to him)* Oh, Master Linton—

EDGAR. Yes, Ellen?

ELLEN. Please, Mr. Linton—I—

EDGAR. What is it, Ellen?

ELLEN. *(Forcing herself to speak)* You must send Heathcliff away.

EDGAR. *(Laughing slightly)* I can't send him away, Ellen. You know that.

ELLEN. But you can forbid him this house— If you don't—

EDGAR. If I don't—?

ELLEN. Some evil will come of it—I know—

EDGAR. I thank you for your warnings—Ellen— *(His tone changes)* though I don't need them.

(EDGAR *goes out through window.* ELLEN *gathers up the papers with which the books were wrapped and puts them in the fireplace.* ISABEL *enters Left. Her eyes are red with weeping and she is sobbing into her handkerchief. Seeing* ELLEN *she controls herself and becomes rather dignified.* ELLEN *eyes her keenly for an instant, then turns and again busies herself with the fire.)*

ISABEL. Build it high, Ellen; I'm cold.

ELLEN. Yes, Miss. I only hope you're not sick.

ISABEL. Sick! What makes you think I'm sick? I said I was cold.

ELLEN. You ate no breakfast.

ISABEL. I wanted none. Oh, I couldn't have swallowed a mouthful—not a mouthful.

ELLEN. *(Disapprovingly)* You're very fretful.

ISABEL. *(Pacing)* Fretful! Oh, fretful you call it! The servants never do what I tell. them—Edgar neglects me—and Catherine lets me do nothing—nothing at all. A slave in my brother's house, that's what I am—a slave. Oh, and I've caught a cold from the doors being left open, and now look—you've let the fire go out on purpose to vex me. Why shouldn't I be fretful? It's a wonder I'm not ill—it's a wonder I'm not dead. *(She sits sofa.)*

ELLEN. I don't know what's been the matter with you lately, Miss Linton. It's not like you to tease and snap for nothing.

ISABEL. For nothing! *Nothing!* Tease—snap! You talk as though I were a child. Everyone treats me like a child—and I'm not.

ELLEN. You're acting like a baby.

ISABEL. *(Rising. Grandly)* Ellen! Enough of your impertinence! I may be despised in my own home, but I am still Isabel Linton.

(CATHERINE, *who has entered Right Center unnoticed, overhears the last few words.*)

CATHERINE. *(In the best of humors)* Isabel, love, you're beginning to talk like a novel. It's comical. Whatever are you doing, Ellen? Put out the fire. It's stifling. Open the doors and let in the sun. *(Throwing open the French window)* Ah, it's such a splendid day and I'm so happy!

ELLEN. Miss Isabel was just complaining of—

CATHERINE. Complaining! Why, there's nothing

to complain of. *(Embracing.* ISABEL*)* I love you,
Isabel. And Ellen—I love you too.

(ELLEN *exits Left.)*

ISABEL. Will you *please* shut that door?

CATHERINE. But it's such a warm day—

ISABEL. Very well—I'll shut it myself. *(She shuts
the window with a bang.* CATHERINE, *unruffled,
moves about singing; looks at self in mirror, up
Center table; trills.)* Where is Edgar?

CATHERINE. *(Carelessly)* Oh, I don't know.
Around somewhere—upstairs, I suppose.

ISABEL. *(Sitting chair down Right)* I don't like
the tone you use when you speak of my brother.

CATHERINE. Why, I love Edgar. He's a darling,
and so are you, Isabel.

ISABEL. I didn't ask your opinion of me.

CATHERINE. But I love you so—I had to give it—

ISABEL. I suppose you're expecting Heathcliff.

CATHERINE. I'm hoping he'll come. We should
have a lovely walk—don't you think so?

ISABEL. I trust you appreciate how nice Edgar's
been.

CATHERINE. About what, may I ask?

ISABEL. About Heathcliff, of course. Edgar
doesn't like him, yet he's never forbidden him to
come here.

CATHERINE. Oh, if that's what you mean—Edgar
couldn't forbid Heathcliff. He couldn't keep Heathcliff from seeing me.

ISABEL. *(Suddenly beginning to sob)* No—I suppose not—

CATHERINE. *(Crossing to* ISABEL*)* What's the
matter with you, Isabel? Haven't we always taken
you on our walks?

ISABEL. Yes—you've *taken* me.

CATHERINE. Why, Isabel, you're crying.

ISABEL. I'm not. *(Sniffling)* I've a cold, that's all.

CATHERINE. I'm glad to know what's wrong with you. *(Moves away)* You've been trying to fight with me all morning. I thought it was bad temper—I'm glad it's only a cold. But, love, you must go straight to bed. It wouldn't do for you to walk with us today.

ISABEL. *(Flaring up)* You shan't get rid of me.

CATHERINE. Get rid of you, child! How can you say such a thing? You really must be sick. Why, you're feverish. Come, I'm going to put you to bed myself.

ISABEL. *(Breaking away)* I won't go to bed. I'm not sick—I haven't even got a cold—I'm perfectly well. It's you—you who're making me miserable.

CATHERINE. I! When?

ISABEL. Yesterday—and now.

CATHERINE. Yesterday? When yesterday? How?

ISABEL. In our walk along the moor. You told me to ramble where I pleased while you walked on with Heathcliff.

CATHERINE. *(Moving above sofa)* How foolish you are! It wasn't that we didn't *want* your company. We didn't care whether you were with us or not. I merely thought Heathcliff's talk would bore you.

ISABEL. Bore me! Oh, no—you sent me away because you knew I wanted to be there.

CATHERINE. Don't be absurd. I'll repeat our conversation word for word, and you shall hear how ordinary it was.

ISABEL. I don't mind the conversation. I wanted to be with—

CATHERINE. Well?

ISABEL. With *him*. And I won't always be sent off. *(Angrily)* You're a dog in the manger, Catherine—you want no one to be loved but yourself!

CATHERINE. You impertinent little cat! *(She*

laughs) But it's too silly—I can't believe you really *like* Heathcliff.

ISABEL. *(Crossing Center. Passionately)* Like him! I love him. I love him better than you ever loved Edgar. And he might love me—if you'd let him.

CATHERINE. *(Coolly)* Do you think so?

ISABEL. Yes.

CATHERINE. *(After a pause, in a changed tone)* I wouldn't be you for a kingdom, then.

ISABEL. What do you mean?

CATHERINE. *(Moving away)* Nothing—

ISABEL. Tell me—what do you mean?

CATHERINE. *(Turning on her)* I mean that Heathcliff is a cruel, desperate man.

ISABEL. He's not. He's an honorable soul—and a true one.

CATHERINE. Oh, you and your talk about souls! What do you know about souls anyway? What do you know about people, for that matter? I tell you Heathcliff is—

ISABEL. I won't listen to you.

CATHERINE. You shall. He's cruel, I say—cruel and merciless.

ISABEL. Cruel! Merciless! How dare you talk like that when you know how good he is? What about Joseph? When nobody would have him, when even the Vicar wanted to send him to the madhouse, Heathcliff took him in. Merciless! I should rather call it noble—Christian.

CATHERINE. Oh, good heavens! Are you utterly blind? Do you really believe he brought Joseph back to Wuthering out of pity?

ISABEL. I do.

CATHERINE. Then you're a fool. There was no pity in it. Listen—he took Joseph in because he likes to see how low an old enemy has fallen,

(Seizes ISABEL'S *arms)* Do you understand me? He likes to watch Joseph, and he likes to hear—

ISABEL. *(Breaking away Left)* Stop! I won't listen to your wicked lies! You want me to think there's no goodness in the world—you want me to see things as you do—darkly.

CATHERINE. I want you to know the truth.

ISABEL. No, you're selfish and wicked. I hate you. You wouldn't say such things of Heathcliff unless you were jealous.

CATHERINE. Jealous of *you!* Heathcliff cares nothing for you—

ISABEL. I know—but he could. He could love me— if you'd let him.

CATHERINE. You think so? Very well. Only I've warned you. After all, you're a mere girl. You can't—

ISABEL. Don't call me a girl. I'm a woman, and I won't have you treat me as if—

(ISABEL *sees the figure of* HEATHCLIFF *appear at the French window and breaks off abruptly. A pause, then* HEATHCLIFF *enters.)*

CATHERINE. *(Gaily)* Heathcliff!

HEATHCLIFF. Good morning!

CATHERINE. Come in. Now, here are two people sadly in need of a third—and you're the one both of us would choose. Isn't that so, Isabel?

ISABEL. *(Eager to escape)* Good morning— But I'm afraid you'll have to excuse me— I—I really must go up and—

CATHERINE. *(Taking* ISABEL'S *arm)* No—stay!

ISABEL. *(Startled)* Catherine!

CATHERINE. Isabel has something to tell you, Heathcliff.

ISABEL. *(Terrified)* Catherine! That's not so. That's—

CATHERINE. *(Lightly)* Heathcliff—I'm proud at last to show you someone who dotes on you more than I do myself.

ISABEL. Catherine!

CATHERINE. Poor little Isabel here is breaking her heart over your moral beauty.

HEATHCLIFF. *(Dryly)* That's very flattering.

CATHERINE. Well, I should say it is! (ISABEL *tries to go, but* CATHERINE *catches her.)* No, you shan't run off. We've been quarreling like cats about you, Heathcliff, and I was quite beaten in vows of devotion.

ISABEL. *(Mortified)* Catherine, I'd thank you to tell the truth. Do let me go.

CATHERINE. By no means! I won't be called a dog in the manger again. You'll stay. Heathcliff—aren't you pleased? Isabel swears my love for Edgar is nothing to that she holds for you. And she has fasted since yesterday's walk because I sent her away.

HEATHCLIFF. *(Who has been watching* ISABEL *keenly)* Now, at any rate, she wishes to go.

(ISABEL, *struggling to get away, scratches* CATHER-INE.)

CATHERINE. Oh! *(Releasing her)* All right—go! (ISABEL *runs out down Left, sobbing. Laughing)* Look, Heathcliff—claws! You must beware of your eyes.

HEATHCLIFF. *(After a pause)* What did you mean by teasing her that way? What you said wasn't true, was it?

CATHERINE. I assure you it was. She's been fascinated by you ever since you came back. I suspected it before, but today she came out in the open. *(Laughing)* But don't notice it. I merely wished to shame her.

HEATHCLIFF. *(Casually)* She's like Linton, isn't she?

CATHERINE. *(Also casually, also trying to discover if he is attracted to* ISABEL*)* Yes—she is— She's pretty—prettier than I am, really. *(A pause)* And have you noticed her eyes?

HEATHCLIFF. No—I haven't.

CATHERINE. You should.

HEATHCLIFF. Are you ready to go?

CATHERINE. *(Picking up her cloak)* Yes. Oh, it's such a glorious day—and Ellen's prepared a lunch for us to take along. We'll stop at the Lodge for it as we go— *(She pauses; mockingly)* Oh, we're forgetting poor little Isabel. She'll be broken-hearted. Shall I call her?

HEATHCLIFF. If you like.

CATHERINE. *(Puzzled)* Do you *want* her to come with us?

HEATHCLIFF. *(Casually)* Yes—why not?

CATHERINE. *(Coldly)* Very well, then. (CATHERINE *crosses toward door Left as though to call* ISABEL. *Suddenly she turns back)* Of course, Heathcliff, you didn't take what I said about Isabel seriously.

HEATHCLIFF. *(Indifferently)* Oh, no.

CATHERINE. It was really unkind of me to tease her. Of course she's young and silly, but you know I'm devoted to her. *(A slight pause)* I just want you to understand that I was only joking—the whole thing's absurd.

HEATHCLIFF. Then why discuss it?

CATHERINE. Naturally she's fond of you, but it's just a girlish infatuation.

HEATHCLIFF. I said why talk about it?

CATHERINE. You don't have to speak to me in that tone of voice— I only meant to say—

HEATHCLIFF. I don't want to talk about her.

CATHERINE. *(Harshly)* I've noticed that.

HEATHCLIFF. Shall we go?

CATHERINE. I don't think I care to go—now.

HEATHCLIFF. Very well. (HEATHCLIFF *makes a slight move toward the window.*)

CATHERINE. *(Sharply)* Heathcliff! *(He turns back.)* You've been unbearable lately.

HEATHCLIFF. Have I?

CATHERINE. Yes. If Isabel could see you as I do, she'd come to her senses, and no mistake.

HEATHCLIFF. *(Insolently)* Would she?

CATHERINE. Your rudeness alone would disgust her.

HEATHCLIFF. My rudeness!

CATHERINE. Yes.

HEATHCLIFF. And since when do I owe you courtesy? You can buy it from your servants, and Edgar has nothing else to give, but don't expect it from me.

CATHERINE. Heathcliff!

HEATHCLIFF. You want me to bow humbly before you—always the unwelcome guest in your husband's house? No, Cathy, I've had too much of it already.

CATHERINE. I'm sorry, Heathcliff. It's difficult for me too—but we are together.

HEATHCLIFF. Not together—apart. We see each other, that's all.

CATHERINE. It's your fault—you won't forgive.

HEATHCLIFF. Forgive!

CATHERINE. I know I treated you badly; but remember, Heathcliff, when I sent you away that night, I also condemned myself.

HEATHCLIFF. *(Harshly)* Condemned yourself!

CATHERINE. Oh, Heathcliff, you've changed so. When you came back, I thought I was going to be happy again, but you've given me only bitterness.

HEATHCLIFF. And what have you given me? A few kind words, and permission to visit the Grange.

CATHERINE. Heathcliff, please—

HEATHCLIFF. You sent me to Hell and you ask me to forget what's burned into me. Well, I can't—and I won't forgive. Some can. That's because they feel nothing. *I can't forgive*, but I can pay back all who have hurt me.

CATHERINE. *(Coldly)* I see. And I suppose you've found satisfaction in Joseph's punishment?

HEATHCLIFF. Yes.

CATHERINE. If Isabel could hear you say that! *(She laughs)* It's a ghastly idea. If people knew, they would think you mad too.

HEATHCLIFF. I don't harm him.

CATHERINE. You're good to him?

HEATHCLIFF. I wouldn't want him to die.

CATHERINE. *(Morbidly curious)* Tell me—is he afraid? Do you think he knows you?

HEATHCLIFF. I think he knows me. He obeys me.

CATHERINE. Well, since I'm to be punished too, what is my fate? Must I share Joseph's—or would you rather hang me by the hair with burning coals at my feet? Isabel has a merry book on tortures. Perhaps you'd like to borrow it!

HEATHCLIFF. People know how to torture without instruction.

CATHERINE. Yes—that's so. *(A pause)* Perhaps I've suffered too—you weren't the only one—

HEATHCLIFF. *(Savagely)* You deserved to suffer, and if you have I'm glad of it. I'd like to make you suffer more—feel all the pain I've felt. *(He grasps her arm.)*

CATHERINE. *(Breaking away)* Go away. You frighten me. I do believe you'd like to hurt me. *(She backs toward the door down Left)* Isabel and I will walk alone today. I'm sorry for the way I treated her in your presence, and I'm going to tell her so now. And you—you had better go.

(CATHERINE *slips out Left. There is a pause, then*

HEATHCLIFF *laughs shortly and picks up his hat. As he goes toward the French window,* ISABEL *appears before him.)*

ISABEL. *(Nervous and embarrassed)* Has Catherine gone?

HEATHCLIFF. Yes.

ISABEL. *(Entering)* Oh, Mr. Heathcliff—I had to speak to you. I— *(A pause—chokingly)* I am so ashamed— I hope you won't think me forward, but those things Catherine said! Oh— *(For a moment she is too overcome to speak. She moves Center)* What must you think of me? *(A pause)* Of course you don't believe what she said?

HEATHCLIFF. It wasn't true?

ISABEL. *(Hesitating)* No— *(Hastily)* Oh, please understand, Mr. Heathcliff, that I do *like* you. And I want to warn you—I must warn you against Catherine. I don't believe the wicked things she said about you—and she did speak against you—but you should know— She's a dangerous friend.

HEATHCLIFF. Catherine doesn't lie, Miss Linton.

ISABEL. She doesn't mean to, but—she can't read character, or she would know— *(Choking with embarrassment)* how kind you are—

HEATHCLIFF. *(Slightly amused)* What makes you think that?

ISABEL. *(With enthusiasm)* Your great devotion to Catherine—and your kindness to poor Joseph. That shows your nobility—and besides, I know it.

HEATHCLIFF. You're a silly girl, Isabel.

ISABEL. But you're not angry with me?

HEATHCLIFF. Why should I be?

ISABEL. Because—because of my boldness—

HEATHCLIFF. *(After a pause)* Cathy didn't tell you I kept Joseph out of mercy—?

ISABEL. No. She said it was because of something else—something terrible.

HEATHCLIFF. Perhaps what she said was true.

ISABEL. No, it wasn't! I *won't* believe that! You're afraid people will think you kind. But—I understand you—Heathcliff—

HEATHCLIFF. Then you would not be afraid to marry me?

ISABEL. Oh— *(A silence. When* ISABEL *speaks again her voice is changed)* You do love me—?

HEATHCLIFF. I ask you to marry me. *(A pause)* You would have to live at Wuthering.

ISABEL. Wuthering is so—romantic—

HEATHCLIFF. You may not think so always. You might as well know that Cathy is right. I'm just as she says. If you marry me I'm afraid you'll be unhappy.

ISABEL. Oh, no, Heathcliff, I could never be unhappy.

HEATHCLIFF. Perhaps not, but some day you may remember I warned you. *(A pause)* Will you come with me now?

ISABEL. *(Surprised and afraid)* Now!

HEATHCLIFF. Yes. You don't expect them to consent, do you? They'll stop us if they can. If you really wish to marry me, it must be at once.

ISABEL. *(Losing her head)* Oh, but I've nothing ready! Why, I—

HEATHCLIFF. You need nothing. You have a cloak. That's enough.

ISABEL. Oh, it would be thrilling! To run away—without telling a soul! And how mad Catherine would be! It would show her, wouldn't it? *(She laughs)* Do you really think we could? Oh, Heathcliff, I can't believe it—I can't!

HEATHCLIFF. Go out at once. I'll follow and meet you at the end of the park. We'll go to Farling till the banns are published.

ISABEL. *(Her courage failing)* No—no, I'm

afraid. I don't dare. Edgar would never forgive me
—never—I know it! And besides, it's wrong.
(CATHERINE'S *voice is heard calling "Isabel."* ISA-
BEL, *continued after a pause)* That nasty cat!
(Fiercely) I hate her! (CATHERINE *calls again.)*
She's coming. Oh, Heathcliff.

(ISABEL *clings to* HEATHCLIFF. CATHERINE *enters
Left. There is a pause; then* ISABEL *slowly
frees herself.)*

CATHERINE. Isabel!
ISABEL. *(Crossing to* CATHERINE*)* I've nothing to
say to you, Catherine. Let me by.

(CATHERINE *steps aside and* ISABEL *goes out Left.*
CATHERINE *closes the door behind* ISABEL *before she speaks.)*

CATHERINE. *(Turning to* HEATHCLIFF; *bitterly)*
Well, Heathcliff!
HEATHCLIFF. Yes, Cathy.
CATHERINE. So you mean to take advantage of
Isabel?
HEATHCLIFF. Don't pretend you care about *her.*
CATHERINE. *(Jealously)* It happens that I do—
very much. What did you say to her?
HEATHCLIFF. What difference?
CATHERINE. *(After a pause)* Tell me—do you
want to marry her?
HEATHCLIFF. Perhaps—
CATHERINE. Why? (HEATHCLIFF *does not an-
swer. Catches her breath)* To hurt me, I suppose?
You think to punish me that way? Well, it's no good
—nothing you do can hurt me now.
HEATHCLIFF. They say a peasant always dreams
of owning land. *(Crossing to windows)* Well, I

dream of one day owning land— I'd like to own the Grange and Wuthering, and all the lands between —all Edgar's land.

CATHERINE. *(Gasping)* I can't believe—

HEATHCLIFF. Quite simply—I covet my neighbor's goods.

CATHERINE. But this neighbor's goods are *mine*.

HEATHCLIFF. They may not be—always.

CATHERINE. You fool—Isabel owns nothing.

HEATHCLIFF. *(Crossing to* CATHERINE*)* As her husband I should have a claim—a strong claim. She's next in line. I intend to get what's owed me— by Edgar and you and all my enemies.

CATHERINE. You call me an enemy? !

HEATHCLIFF. Yes.

CATHERINE. *(Moves down; sinks on stool Center)* Oh, why did you ever come back? When you were gone I at least had your memory. I knew that somewhere in the world there was someone I loved, but now—now I have nothing— (HEATHCLIFF *goes to her. There is a silence. For an instant they are again close to one another.* HEATHCLIFF *softly whispers her name and bends toward her. Suddenly* CATHERINE'S *anger flares anew. She rises; breaks Right)* Don't touch me, and get out of my house. You'll never see Isabel again. I'll send her away—some place where you can't find her. Isabel may love you, but I'd rather see her dead than your wife.

EDGAR. *(The door suddenly opens and* EDGAR *enters Left. Feigning surprise)* Well, Cathy, I didn't expect to find you here. Ellen told me you'd planned to walk to Duxton Ridge.

CATHERINE. No, we've decided not to. Heathcliff is going.

EDGAR. *(Closing door)* Really? I'm surprised— I understand you were looking forward to it with such pleasure—

CATHERINE. Yes, I was.

HEATHCLIFF. Goodbye, Cathy.

EDGAR. Just a moment. Heathcliff.

HEATHCLIFF. Yes?

EDGAR. I want to talk to you.

CATHERINE. What is it, Edgar?

EDGAR. Just a little matter I want to have settled.

HEATHCLIFF. Very well. What is it?

EDGAR. I'll be frank—

CATHERINE. Please.

EDGAR. *(To* HEATHCLIFF*)* I was in the hallway just now—and I couldn't help overhearing Catherine's last words to you.

CATHERINE. *(Breaking Right)* Oh, you were? Are you sure you weren't listening at the door, Edgar?

EDGAR. *(Ignoring* CATHERINE*)* So far I have been patient, Heathcliff, but there are limits.

HEATHCLIFF. Limits?

EDGAR. Yes—if you have been using your visits to the Grange merely as a pretext to impose yourself upon my sister—

CATHERINE. His visits to *me* as a pretext! Oh, Edgar, you are stupid. You may as well know it— Isabel's infatuated with him, and has been from the start.

EDGAR. I won't believe that—not for one moment. *(To* HEATHCLIFF*)* Nevertheless, I forbid you this house. As you know, I've never liked you, but after what has passed I realize that your presence is a moral poison which—

CATHERINE. Oh, Edgar, must you always make speeches?

EDGAR. Silence, Catherine!—I merely wish to make it clear that you are not to visit the Grange again—and if you do—I shall have you thrown out.

CATHERINE. That's very brave of you, dear, but,

if, as you say, you overheard my last words, you must realize that I've saved you that trouble.

HEATHCLIFF. Yes, Edgar, Catherine has saved you that trouble. I've no reason to come here again —and I promise you I never shall. *(To* CATHERINE*)* Goodbye. *(He smiles, bows slightly, and goes out French window.)*

EDGAR. *(Moves to the mantel. Ironically)* Well, I'm glad to see that you've at last discovered the true character of your "friend." *(Pulls bell cord at mantelpiece.)*

CATHERINE. I've also discovered the true character of my husband.

EDGAR. I don't believe you have. You see, Catherine, I'm still not quite as great a fool as you think. *(A pause)* I know that you love Heathcliff.

CATHERINE. What makes you so sure?

EDGAR. For one thing your jealousy of Isabel.

CATHERINE. My jealousy of Isabel! Why, it's perfectly obvious that I was only protecting her.

EDGAR. You sent him away, I'll admit. But I'm not certain that you did it wholly for love of my sister. *(A pause)* Yes, Catherine, you love Heathcliff. Perhaps that's your curse, just as mine is loving you.

ELLEN. *(Enters Left)* You rang, sir?

EDGAR. Yes, Ellen. Go find Isabel and ask her to come here at once.

(ELLEN *goes out Left.)*

CATHERINE. And what do you want of Isabel?

EDGAR. *(Crossing Center to* CATHERINE*)* It's entirely natural that I should want to speak to her at this time, isn't it? I intend to hear directly from her whether or not there's any truth in this ridiculous tale.

CATHERINE. *(Sarcastically)* And what if she admits it?   *(WARN Curtain.)*

EDGAR. In that case, since neither of us apparently wishes the affair to go any farther, it might be to our mutual advantage to dissuade her.

ELLEN. *(Hurries in Left, an unfolded sheet of paper in her hand)* She's gone! I found this— Oh, Mr. Linton—

EDGAR. *(Unbelieving)* Gone—

CATHERINE. *(Crossing to* ELLEN; *seizing the note)* Let me have it. (CATHERINE *reads the note)* Yes, Edgar—they've gone!

EDGAR. I can't believe—

CATHERINE. Read this.

EDGAR. *(Turning away upstage)* No— No, I won't read it. *(A pause.)*

CATHERINE. *(Controlling her anger)* Well, Edgar, what are you going to do?

ELLEN. They can't have gone far.

CATHERINE. No—that's true. They must still be within the Park. Run, Ellen, and send the servants to catch them while there's still time.

(ELLEN *hurries to door Left.)*

EDGAR. No, Ellen.

ELLEN. *(Stopping)* But, Mr. Linton—

EDGAR. No, Ellen—let her go.

CATHERINE. Edgar!

EDGAR. She went of her own accord—she had a right to go if she pleased. We'll trouble no more about her.

CATHERINE. *(Crossing to* EDGAR*)* But, Edgar—

EDGAR. You heard what I said, Catherine. *(He takes* CATHERINE *gently by the hand)* We'll trouble no more about them.

CURTAIN

ACT TWO

SCENE III

The same. Midnight—a night in winter.

The empty room is lighted only by a faint glow from the fire, which has been banked for the night. The curtains are drawn at the windows.

After a pause, CATHERINE, *wearing a dressing gown, steals into the room from Left. She has risen from a sick bed and is obviously weak. She closes the door cautiously, then suddenly crosses to the French window, tears the curtains apart, and tries to open the windows. They are locked. Her strength fails. She leans against window and murmurs* HEATHCLIFF'S *name faintly. She wanders to the fire and begins to poke at it idly. It begins to flare, and she appears to come to life with it. Moving lightly, almost like a child, she goes to the sofa, gathers up the pillows, returns and spreads them before the fire.*

CATHERINE. *(As she sinks down on pillows)* Burn, little fire, burn. *(She pokes the fire)* Banked with ashes, you're almost dead— *(The fire flares again)* There!

(CATHERINE *stretches out happily before the fire. There is a pause, then* CATHERINE *hears a SOUND from within. She sits bolt upright and, as one hunted, presses back against the fireplace, partly hidden by the shadows.* ELLEN, *also in dressing gown, and carrying a lighted candle, enters Left.)*

ELLEN. *(Calling softly)* Cathy! Cathy! (CATHER-INE *does not answer.* ELLEN *sees the parted curtains, the pillows before the fire, and then* CATHERINE. ELLEN *hurries to her. Dropping to her knees beside* CATHERINE*)* Catherine—my little girl—

CATHERINE. *(Her arms about* ELLEN, *sweetly)* Ellen—

ELLEN. *(Getting her breath)* Ah, what a turn you gave me. I heard a step in the hall, and when I went to your room you weren't there. I was terrified. I thought you might have gone—

CATHERINE. Gone where?

ELLEN. *(Severely)* Never mind. I'm an old woman now and you mustn't play such tricks on me, ma'am.

CATHERINE. *(Innocently)* I play no tricks, Ellen.

ELLEN. *(Picking up a pillow)* You've been so ill. Now come up to bed at once.

CATHERINE. *(Gaily)* I won't. I won't. I won't. *(Grabs the pillow. It tears a little, and a few feathers fall.)*

ELLEN. Ah, Cathy, now you've torn it!

CATHERINE. Good. I'll tear them all—till the parlor is knee deep in feathers—like snow.

ELLEN. Come with me, Cathy—or I'll call the master.

CATHERINE. No, Ellen, I'll call him myself— I'll scream and awake the whole household. Shall I do that?

ELLEN. *(Hurrying to door Left and shutting it)* Cathy, be quiet.

CATHERINE. *(Laughing)* There, I knew you didn't mean it. Now come back to me, dear. I want you to sit by me. (ELLEN *does not move.)* Doctor Kenneth said I wasn't to be crossed, you know.

ELLEN. But, Cathy—

CATHERINE. And the room's so warm and I feel

so well and I'm happy here. You'll break my heart if you send me to bed.

ELLEN. *(Relenting)* Ah, Cathy—

CATHERINE. Now light the candles, and sit beside me. (ELLEN *lights another candle.* CATHERINE'S *voice is changed)* How long have I been shut up in that room, Ellen?

ELLEN. I'm sure it's weak of me to humor you—

CATHERINE. And now it's winter—only a few weeks—it must be more— I feel as though I had been shut up for years. *(She begins sorting out some of the feathers which have fallen from the pillow. She speaks as though to herself)* This is a wild duck's—and this a pigeon's— And here is a moorcock's, and this—I'd know it among a thousand— it's a lapwing's. Lovely bird, wheeling above our heads in the middle of the heath! It wanted to get to its nest, for the clouds had touched the hills and it felt rain coming. This feather was picked up from the heath—the bird wasn't shot—we saw its nest in winter, full of little skeletons. Heathcliff had set a trap over it and the old ones dared not come. I made him promise he'd never shoot a lapwing after that, and he didn't—

ELLEN. Stop your nonsense.

CATHERINE. *(With sudden passion—rising)* Oh, I wish I were out of doors. I wish I were a girl again, half savage, and strong and free, laughing at pain, not maddening under it. *(Sitting beside* EL-LEN*)* Why am I changed—why does my blood rush into a hell of tumult at a few words? I'm sure I'd be myself were I out there. *(Rising)* Open the window wide—Ellen. Fasten it open. Quickly.

ELLEN. *(Rising)* And give you your death of cold.

CATHERINE. Give me my chance of life, you mean. *I'll* open it. *(She runs toward window.)*

ELLEN. No.

CATHERINE. *(Stopping Center)* Look! The lights at Wuthering!

ELLEN. Catherine, come to bed. There are no lights.

CATHERINE. I see them. That's my room with the candle in it and the trees swaying before the window, and the other candle is in Joseph's garret and the wind is sounding in the firs by the lattice. Do let me feel it—it comes straight down the moor. *(Crosses to window)* Do let me have one breath. (CATHERINE *struggles with* ELLEN, *trying to unlock the window.)*

ELLEN. *(Restraining her)* No. (CATHERINE *breaks away with a faint cry of desperation.)* I'll call the master. (ELLEN *crosses toward the Left door. Suddenly* CATHERINE *screams.)* Catherine!

(WARN Curtain.)

CATHERINE. *(Pointing to a small mirror on wall near* ELLEN*)* Don't you see that face?

ELLEN. Cathy, dearest. It's only the mirror. *(Covers mirror with her little shawl.)*

CATHERINE. It's behind there still, and it stirred. I hope it won't come out when you're gone. Oh, Nelly, the room is haunted. I'm afraid to be alone.

ELLEN. Come up to bed and sleep.

CATHERINE. *(Sinking onto the stool Center)* I thought I was at home. I thought I was lying asleep in my room at Wuthering. I got confused and screamed. Don't say anything, but stay with me.

ELLEN. *(Standing above* CATHERINE*)* Yes, dear.

CATHERINE. And you won't call Edgar.

ELLEN. No, Child, no.

CATHERINE. *(After a pause)* Why doesn't he come to me?

ELLEN. *(Faintly)* Who?

CATHERINE. Heathcliff.

ELLEN. Don't, Cathy, don't. *(A pause.)*

CATHERINE. I won't die, will I, Nell?

ELLEN. No, dear.

CATHERINE. I used to believe I couldn't die. Heathcliff and I often braved the ghosts in the churchyard, standing together among the graves, daring them to appear.

ELLEN. Catherine, come to bed.

CATHERINE. They may bury me twelve feet deep and throw the church down over me, *(Rising)* but I'll not rest till you're with me, Heathcliff. I never will.

CURTAIN

ACT THREE

SCENE: *The living-room of Wuthering Heights. Morning, the following spring.*
    The room, though furnished as in Act One, is dirty and ill-kept. The pewter plate has lost its luster, dust lies over everything.

AT RISE: ISABEL *is looking out of window up Right. She seems much older. Her dress is untidy, and her unwashed hair hangs in wisps about her ears.*
    HEATHCLIFF *is seated at a small table on the other side of the room. He is studying in an open book, and writing. He is neatly dressed and looks well.*

HEATHCLIFF. *(When he speaks there is a distinct note of contempt in his voice)* You've been watching at that window all morning. Are you expecting someone?

ISABEL. *(Stammering)* No—no.

HEATHCLIFF. Then why do you do it?

ISABEL. I suppose I'm *allowed* to look out, aren't I? I like to—that's why I'm doing it. Besides, with the rains over, I can see the Grange again. *(A pause)* How white and far away it looks!

HEATHCLIFF. You get a good deal of joy out of weeping for your old home, don't you?

ISABEL. *(Turning on him; fretfully)* And what else can I do; you've ruined my life—

HEATHCLIFF. Perhaps if you weren't such a slattern you could make a life for yourself here. You used to think Wuthering romantic enough.

ISABEL. *(In the same whining tone)* I hadn't lived here then. I didn't know what it was like—how cold, or how it whispers with every wind. It's a ghastly place, and I hate it.

HEATHCLIFF. It'd be better if you'd clean it up.

ISABEL. *(With dignity)* I'm accustomed to being served, not serving.

HEATHCLIFF. All right—squat in your own filth. Look at your hair! It isn't even washed. You're getting to be a dirty—

ISABEL. *(Crossing at him; angrily)* Don't talk like that to me. I won't stand it. Some day you'll drive me to the point where—

HFATHCLIFF. *(Pleasantly)* Would you like to see my studies?

ISABEL. I would not.

HEATHCLIFF. I write a good hand, don't I—for one who's taught himself?

ISABEL. Writing! As though that were anything to be proud of.

HEATHCLIFF. I'm proud of it, none the less. Get back to the window—you're in my light there.

ISABEL. I won't be ordered around. Heathcliff, I want to talk to you—seriously.

HEATHCLIFF. Yes? *(Writes.)*

ISABEL. I want to tell you I know you've treated me badly. I—

HEATHCLIFF. Oh, if that's all—

ISABEL. Didn't I give up everything for you—everything? Think what I had—home, love, servants—and I gave them all up—and for what?

HEATHCLIFF. *(Still writing; with exasperating indifference)* What?

ISABEL. *(Furious)* I'll stand no more of your insolence! Listen to me! *(He continues to write.)*

Stop writing! I'm talking to you—stop, I say! *(She dashes the papers from the desk.)*

HEATHCLIFF. *(Catching her wrist)* Damn you!

ISABEL. *(Clinging to him fiercely)* Love me! Love me, Heathcliff!

HEATHCLIFF. Get away!

ISABEL. *(Throwing arms about him)* Hurt me—love me—anything—only don't treat me as though I were—

HEATHCLIFF. *(Shaking her off)* Get off me—you—you common little slut! *(He throws her down on the sofa. She weeps bitterly.)*

ISABEL. Oh, God—I wish I were dead. (HEATHCLIFF *gathers up papers and moves table.)* If only you were good to me, but I can't bear to have you hate me. What is my life?—exile! Even the townspeople don't speak to me now.

HEATHCLIFF. At one time you didn't speak to them.

ISABEL. The peasants! Not that I care because they cut me! They aren't good enough for me to spit on.

HEATHCLIFF. You're not so ladylike as you used to be, are you?

ISABEL. I'm so terribly unhappy—

HEATHCLIFF. *(At fireplace)* Is that what you said in the letter you sent to the Grange Thursday?

ISABEL. *(Affecting surprise)* I sent no letter.

HEATHCLIFF. What's the use of lying? You sent a letter to the Grange by little Harvey. I saw you give it to him.

ISABEL. Well, what if I did? I wrote to Ellen.

HEATHCLIFF. Are you sure you didn't write to your brother?

ISABEL. If you must know, I have. But he never answered.

HEATHCLIFF. So you told Ellen how miserable you are—what a bad husband I am.

ISABEL. How did you know? You read my letter!

HEATHCLIFF. *(Crossing Right)* Why should I read it? That's the way you always complain. Why shouldn't you say the same thing to Ellen? I suppose you also asked her to come here?

ISABEL. *(Rising. Angry)* You read my letter!

HEATHCLIFF. No, I didn't read it. But I did notice you watching at the window all morning.

ISABEL. All right—I was watching—for Ellen! I'm desperate! I'll go mad if I don't see someone from home.

HEATHCLIFF. What if I don't let Ellen in?

ISABEL. You'll let her in—I'm certain of that.

HEATHCLIFF. What makes you so sure?

ISABEL. *(Moving toward him)* Because you want to see her as much as I do. If I've been cut away from my world, so have you from yours. You'd like to know about Catherine, wouldn't you? *(A pause)* Oh, I know you still love her—you don't hide it from me. That's why you'll let Ellen in. You want to see her too—and you want to know if Catherine is going to die—as people say—

HEATHCLIFF. Stop it! Stop!

(From upstairs comes a distant and muffled POUNDING.)

ISABEL. *(Her nerves on edge—breaks Left)* Oh, that monster—that monster—why don't you kill him? I can't stand it—I can't! That sound—day and night!

HEATHCLIFF. There's a lot you can't stand.

(The POUNDING ceases.)

ISABEL. Why don't you kill him? Horrible gibbering idiot! Why should such a thing live?

HEATHCLIFF. You once thought me noble because I took Joseph in.

ISABEL. I was a fool. Now I know better. You let him live for the same reason you let me live— and it's not mercy. You want to hurt everyone— Catherine, Edgar and me—but me most of all.

HEATHCLIFF. Be quiet! I'm sick of listening to you.

ISABEL. *(Moving Center)* And I won't be told—

HEATHCLIFF. Shut up!

ISABEL. See if I obey you! I'll talk till I rot if I wish.

HEATHCLIFF. You dirty little—

(There is a KNOCKING without.)

ISABEL. That's Ellen— I'll go.

HEATHCLIFF. Stay. I'll see who it is. *(He goes to door Right.* ISABEL *smooths her hair and awaits nervously.* HEATHCLIFF *admits* ELLEN*)* We expected you. Come in.

ELLEN. *(Stiffly)* Thank you, I'm sure.

ISABEL. *(Taking her hand)* It's so good to see you, Ellen. Come over here and give me your things. *(Drawing her Left, away from* HEATHCLIFF. *Whispers)* Ellen, have you a letter for me?

HEATHCLIFF. If you have anything for Isabel, give it to her. You needn't make a secret of it. We have no secrets between us.

ELLEN. I have nothing.

ISABEL. *(Crosses down Right)* Oh, Ellen!

ELLEN. Your brother bid me say you must expect no letter or visit from him. He sends his love, ma'am, and his best wishes for your happiness— also his pardon, but he thinks this household and his should not communicate, as nothing could come of it.

ISABEL. *(Sits Right)* Oh—

HEATHCLIFF. *(Sarcastically)* Why haven't you come to see us before, Ellen?

ELLEN. *(Still coldly)* Mrs. Linton's illness has occupied all my time.

HEATHCLIFF. *(Faltering)* Oh—

ELLEN. *(Crosses to settle)* I am only here today because Mr. Linton said I might come—to deliver his message.

HEATHCLIFF. You let Edgar bully you, don't you?

ELLEN. *(Sits)* I'd be a poor servant were I disloyal to my master. You've done him an evil turn, Heathcliff, and need not think my sympathy lies with you. I came to see Isabel.

HEATHCLIFF. But you're going to talk to me— about Catherine—

ELLEN. She's been very ill.

HEATHCLIFF. I know that—I know *that!* Tell me about her! Tell me!

ELLEN. She's able to move about the house at last, but she's only just recovering. God be thanked her life is spared. *(Sharply)* And if you've any love for her, you'll not cross her way again.

HEATHCLIFF. Ellen—

ELLEN. I mean it. You're to blame. The day you took Isabel away the old fever returned. It nearly burned out her brain. It was even more terrible than before.

HEATHCLIFF. *(Turning away up stage)* Oh, God!

ISABEL. *(Vacantly)* Is my brother well?

ELLEN. Yes—but I'm afraid he misses you greatly.

ISABEL. *(Brightening)* Do you think so?

ELLEN. He never says so directly, but I feel it. Ah, the last months have been a nightmare! Catherin's not an easy patient—she's been more harsh and wilful than ever. I must admit she treats your brother very badly.

ISABEL. She always was ungrateful.

ELLEN. *(Wearily)* But now it's worse— I'm certain he endures her only because of his humanity and sense of duty.

HEATHCLIFF. *(Forcing himself to be calm)* That's possible! It's quite possible that Edgar should have nothing but a sense of duty to fall back on. Oh, I've no doubt she's in hell among you.

ISABEL. Heathcliff!

HEATHCLIFF. *(Pacing)* God, I've waited too long already— I've got to see her.

ELLEN. Never! You shan't see her again—now that she's nearly forgotten you.

HEATHCLIFF. Forgotten me!

ELLEN. Your name is never mentioned at the Grange.

HEATHCLIFF. Forgotten me! And because no one mentions my name! You know that for every thought she gives to Linton there are a thousand for me. Forgotten! I used to believe we could forget each other. I put oceans between us, but we did not forget. The thought that I might pass out of her life finally drove me back, but the night I saw her face again I knew she had not forgotten. I was mad to think she ever could love Linton.

ISABEL. I won't hear my brother belittled in silence.

HEATHCLIFF. *(Crossing down to ISABEL)* He's wondrous fond of you, isn't he? He turns you away with surprising coldness.

ISABEL. He doesn't know how unhappy I am.

HEATHCLIFF. I thought you wrote.

ISABEL. I didn't tell him that— I only asked him to forgive me.

HEATHCLIFF. *(To ELLEN)* But she did tell you?

ELLEN. Yes. She wrote about her miserable life here, but Mr. Linton didn't read the letter. He said Isabel had made her choice. *(Coldly)* What she wrote seems to be more true than I thought. My young lady is looking sadly the worse.

HEATHCLIFF. *(Crossing to window)* She suits this house better for not being over nice.

ELLEN. You must let her have a maid, and you must treat her more kindly. Whatever you think of Mr. Linton, you can't doubt that Isabel loved you. Why else would she have left her home for such a wilderness as this?

HEATHCLIFF. I owe her nothing. I warned her what life with me would be.

ELLEN. That's no excuse. She was foolish and—

HEATHCLIFF. Can I help that? Is it my fault if that mean-minded brach dreamed I could love her? Tell your master, Nell, that I never saw such a slavish thing—she even disgraces the name of Linton.

ELLEN. *(Shocked)* Heathcliff, I—!

(ISABEL *begins to sob.*)

HEATHCLIFF. I thought she had begun to know me—I hadn't noticed those smiles that disgusted me at first—but only today she begged me to love her.

ISABEL. Oh, I hate you—I hate you!

HEATHCLIFF. *(Above her. Brutally)* Are you sure of that? If I let you alone for a day, won't you come sighing and wheedling to me again? Won't you come back cringing for some brutality, hoping I'll crack a whip over your shoulders?

ELLEN. *(Rising)* Heathcliff—you must be mad.

ISABEL. Take care, Ellen—he's not human—

(From upstairs, POUNDING is heard again. A silence.)

ELLEN. That—that sound—

ISABEL. Oh, go up and stop him—don't let him
do it again.

ELLEN. What was it?

HEATHCLIFF. That was Joseph.

ISABEL. *(Rising)* Don't let him do it again.

ELLEN. Oh, it's ghastly!

HEATHCLIFF. Isabel and I are used to it. We don't
notice. (HEATHCLIFF *mounts the stairs and disappears.)*

ELLEN. Oh, he is wicked!

ISABEL. *(Eager for sympathy—crossing to* EL-
LEN*)* Of course—of course.

ELLEN. Does he—strike you?

ISABEL. No, he doesn't strike me—he doesn't do
that. He loathes me—I'm repulsive to him—he
doesn't even want to touch me. No, he doesn't beat
me, but I wish he would—I wish he would. I wish
he'd beat me—beat me till I couldn't breathe.

ELLEN. *(Alarmed)* Isabel—Isabel! Don't—you're
talking as wildly as he.

ISABEL. Is it any wonder? *(She sobs bitterly.)*

ELLEN. *(Soothing her)* Isabel—dearest—come, be
quiet. Please, dear—

ISABEL. Oh, I can't—I can't—

ELLEN. There, there—that's better— (ISABEL'S
sobs lessen.) Now be still while I fix you a cup of
tea. And after that I'll tidy up the house a bit.
(ELLEN *looks about)* Dear, the place *is* dreadful.
I'd never know it for the house I used to keep.
(ELLEN *starts to get up.)*

ISABEL. *(Restraining her)* No—stay. I want you
to promise you'll not repeat a word of what you've
heard to Edgar. Whatever he pretends, he only
wants to hurt Edgar.

ELLEN. But your brother must be told. He'll take
you away.

ISABEL. *(With conscious self-sacrifice)* No, Ellen,
I forbid you to tell him. Heathcliff only married me

to gain power over Edgar, and he shan't. I'll die first.

ELLEN. Your brother has a right to know, and it's my duty to tell him.

ISABEL. No, Ellen, promise me—promise me you won't tell.

ELLEN. I'll promise nothing.

ISABEL. Ellen—I beg you.

ELLEN. But why—why? I see no reason. Don't you want to leave Heathcliff?

ISABEL. *(After a pause—rising)* No. I don't want to leave him. I admit it.

ELLEN. *(Amazed)* Isabel—I don't understand— Then why did you write me that letter?

ISABEL. *(At fireplace)* I don't know— Perhaps because I was weak and needed your pity. Oh, I *am* unhappy, but, Ellen, don't you see, I love Heathcliff—I love him. Can I help it if I do?

ELLEN. You love him!

ISABEL. Yes. And I can't escape. God knows I've tried, but I can't. It's as though he'd laid a spell on me—

ELLEN. *(Fearfully)* Oh—

ISABEL. I am a slavish thing. It's the truth— I'd do anything to make him love me, but he never will. Catherine has his heart, and I can never take it from her. How I hate her for that! (ELLEN *rises abruptly.)* Ellen—

ELLEN. I'll not stay longer in this house.

ISABEL. Oh, don't go—please—

HEATHCLIFF. *(Re-enters. From the staircase)* You're not going yet, Ellen?

ELLEN. *(Hurriedly)* Yes—I must.

HEATHCLIFF. *(Descending)* You'd better stay. You can't go back without tea.

(There is a KNOCK on the Right door.)

ELLEN. *(Catching her breath)* Who can that be?

ISABEL. *(Also startled)* I don't know. *(The KNOCK is repeated.)* No one visits us—no one—

ELLEN. The master, perhaps—he knew I was coming.

HEATHCLIFF. I'll see. *(He goes out Right.)*

ISABEL. *(Flustered)* Not Edgar—it couldn't be. I couldn't bear to face him.

(CATHERINE, radiant, a small bouquet in her hand, appears at the doorway. HEATHCLIFF, hardly able to believe his eyes, stands behind her. He has grasped her hand. Both ISABEL and ELLEN exclaim.)

HEATHCLIFF. *(Elated)* Look, Ellen—and you told me she was sick!

CATHERINE. *(To ELLEN and ISABEL)* You must be surprised—but is it so dreadful? *(Laughs)* Isabel—I don't believe you're glad to see me.

ELLEN. *(Finding her tongue)* Catherine—you shouldn't have done this. *(Hurrying to her side)* How did you get here? Are you all right?

HEATHCLIFF. Of course she is—can't you see?

ELLEN. *(Brushing him aside)* Be quiet. *(To CATHERINE)* How did you get here?

CATHERINE. I walked.

ELLEN. You walked!

CATHERINE. *(Laughing)* I was always a good walker, wasn't I, Heathcliff?

ELLEN. Oh, dear—you've walked all that way—scarcely up from a sick bed.

CATHERINE. Don't scold, Ellen. It's done me good. And there was a soft wind. It's really warm. I'm only a little tired—

HEATHCLIFF. Sit here, Cathy.

CATHERINE. No—no—let me stand.

ELLEN. What will your husband say?

CATHERINE. He needn't know. I waited till he'd gone to the village before I slipped out. I was sure you were coming here, Ellen— I knew it even though you wouldn't tell.

ISABEL. You had not right to do it, Catherine. Edgar will be terribly worried.

CATHERINE. *(Crossing to ISABEL)* Oh, Isabel, I've brought you these. The earliest flowers on the Heights! *(Offers flowers.)*

ISABEL. Why have you come here?

CATHERINE. Don't be angry, Isabel. Won't you take them?

ISABEL. I don't want your flowers.

HEATHCLIFF. *(Menacing)* Isabel—

CATHERINE. *(Drawing back)* How changed you are!

ISABEL. You needn't make fun of me—just because my dress is old.

CATHERINE. I didn't mean that.

ISABEL. Oh, yes, you did. I know I look horrible, but I didn't expect *you* to see me. We haven't bothered you—why should you bother us? I don't care if you have been sick—I've no sympathy for you. Ellen's told me how you treat my brother—and right now you're deceiving him. You—with your smiles and flowers—oh, I know you!

HEATHCLIFF. Get out of the room.

ISABEL. I won't. I won't.

HEATHCLIFF. Up those stairs!

ISABEL. *(Slipping past him)* I won't go up there! Let me out! *(At door to kitchen—up Left)* You'll be sorry—both of you—I promise you that. *(She goes out.)*

CATHERINE. *(Lets the flowers fall to table Right. Her radiant mood is gone. Dully)* Ah, what can she do?

HEATHCLIFF. Let her go. Are you really all right? Tell me—

ELLEN. See, Catherine, your coming has caused only trouble. Oh, how could you do such a rash thing?

CATHERINE. Yes—I might have known it— But I did want to see the old house—and I wanted to walk on the heath.

ELLEN. Such nonsense!

HEATHCLIFF. I'm glad you've come, Cathy.

ELLEN. *(Taking* CATHERINE *to sofa. To* HEATH-CLIFF*)* No—don't torment her—she must lie down and rest.

CATHERINE. I don't want to lie down.

ELLEN. Obey me! You'll be lucky if you're not in bed a month on account of this. Now I'm going to fix something for you to drink. And after that, Heathcliff, we must drive her back.

CATHERINE. *(Trying to control herself)* Never mind, Ellen. I want nothing.

ELLEN. Do as I say—I know best. Remember you've been very sick.

CATHERINE. *(Her nerves snapping)* Will you never stop nagging? Oh, you with your teas and herbs! I wish you'd go away and let me have a little peace.

ELLEN. *(Tearfully)* You've no right to talk to me so. It's unkind and unjust and I— (ELLEN'S *voice is choked with sobs. She bows her head and goes into the kitchen up Left.)*

CATHERINE. There—I've hurt her—and I didn't want to. I wonder why I always hurt those I love— I'll call her back and tell her I didn't mean it. El-len— *(Rises. Suddenly becomes faint.)*

HEATHCLIFF. *(Alarmed)* Catherine!

CATHERINE. It's nothing—just a sensation—it goes away— I felt it twice while I was walking. *(Laughs)* I wanted to lie down on the heath—the way I used to when I was a girl, but I didn't because it was damp and I couldn't spoil my dress. Now I wish I had. I never used to care about dresses, did I? There—it's quite gone.

HEATHCLIFF. *(Sitting beside her)* I hope it won't come back. For a moment you were so pale.

CATHERINE. It will. *(Laughing)* But I'm not pale any more.

HEATHCLIFF. Only a little.

CATHERINE. *(Discovers one of the sheets of paper on which* HEATHCLIFF *has been writing)* Heathcliff.

HEATHCLIFF. It's nothing.

CATHERINE. My name—over and over—

HEATHCLIFF. I'm learning to write. I was practicing.

CATHERINE. Oh!

HEATHCLIFF. Catherine Ernshaw—a good name to practice on.

CATHERINE. Yes—and you write very well—

HEATHCLIFF. *(No longer able to restrain himself, suddenly falls on his knees before* CATHERINE *and buries his head in her lap. His voice unsteady)* Oh, Cathy, my darling, Cathy— (CATHERINE *runs her fingers through his hair. Her manner is, however, more despairing than tender)* We've been apart so long— (CATHERINE *laughs nervously.)* It was for me you came, wasn't it?

CATHERINE. Yes—I suppose so—

HEATHCLIFF. I wanted to come to you.

CATHERINE. Why didn't you?

HEATHCLIFF. I couldn't return to the Grange—after what had happened.

CATHERINE. No—no, you couldn't. *(She laughs coldly.)*

HEATHCLIFF. *(Looking at her)* Don't laugh like that.

CATHERINE. Why not?

HEATHCLIFF. It's like ice.

CATHERINE. Perhaps.

HEATHCLIFF. Can't you guess what I have suffered without you?

CATHERINE. *(Stiffening)* Suffered—you suffered. Why shouldn't you suffer? (HEATHCLIFF *starts in surprise and attempts to rise.* CATHERINE *seizes him fiercely)* No—stay! I'll hold you— I wish I could hold you until we were both dead.

HEATHCLIFF. Cathy—

CATHERINE. You were the one who left me—and now you talk of suffering—as though you were the one to be pitied. I shan't pity you, not I. How strong you are! How many years you'll live after I'm dead!

HEATHCLIFF. Do you want to drive me mad?

CATHERINE. *(Harshly)* You know I am going to die, don't you?

HEATHCLIFF. It's not true! Ellen said—

CATHERINE. Ellen knows nothing—it's I who know.

HEATHCLIFF. How?

CATHERINE. I overheard Doctor Kenneth. He was talking with Edgar—

HEATHCLIFF. You were delirious. You imagined.

CATHERINE. *(Pressing her breast; fiercely)* And do I also imagine what I *feel*—here?

HEATHCLIFF. Cathy!

CATHERINE. *(Coldly)* I should be almost glad—if I thought it would make you suffer.

HEATHCLIFF. Don't!

CATHERINE. But I wonder if you would. You'd probably say: "Catherine Ernshaw? Oh, I loved her once and was wretched to lose her, but it is past."

HEATHCLIFF. *(Seizing her roughly and lifting her)* I could as soon forget you as my life, and you know it. You want to make me writhe in hell, don't you?

(HEATHCLIFF *pushes her away and staggers to the*

mantel. CATHERINE *sinks back on the sofa.*
HEATHCLIFF *leans against the mantelpiece, his
head hidden by his hand, as though to ward off
a blow. After a silence,* CATHERINE *speaks:)*

CATHERINE. Heathcliff—I'm sorry. I didn't mean
what I said—I swear I didn't. I only wish us never
to be parted. Come here— Won't you come here
again? Do!

(He does not stir. CATHERINE *struggles to her feet
and is about to go to him when he turns and
sees her. With a sudden exclamation he gathers
her into his arms. They kiss passionately.)*

HEATHCLIFF. How beautiful you are! *(His grasp
tightening)* And how cruel!
CATHERINE. You're hurting me.
HEATHCLIFF. You loved. Then what right had
you to leave me? *(Passionately)* Misery and death—
nothing that God could inflict would have parted us
—but *you,* you of your own free will did it—*you!*
CATHERINE. Let me alone! Let me alone!
HEATHCLIFF. *(Fiercely)* Why did you do it—
why did you despise me—why did you betray your
own heart?
CATHERINE. Oh, I'm sorry I came—sorry I ever
saw you again. Let me go. Let me go. *(She breaks
away Right.)*
HEATHCLIFF. *(Following)* Why did you betray
your own heart? Answer me!
CATHERINE. *(Wildly)* I don't know. That's what
I've asked myself a thousand times, but I can't
answer—I can't tell. I only know I couldn't help
myself. *(A pause.* CATHERINE *sinks into chair
Right)* Oh, why do we torture each other? Why
does our love turn to hate? I'm so weary of hate—
HEATHCLIFF. *(After a pause; in a changed voice)*

I had no right to blame you, Cathy; the fault was mine also. *(A pause)* There is only one thing to do now.

CATHERINE. What?

HEATHCLIFF. Will you leave your husband and come to me?

CATHERINE. *(After a pause, dully)* And what of Isabel?

HEATHCLIFF. Let her go where she wants—let her go back to her brother. We're not of their world —no more than the open moor is—and we never will be.

CATHERINE. *(Taking his hand)* Wuthering is our home.

HEATHCLIFF. You will stay?

CATHERINE. *(After a pause; tensely)* Yes—yes, I'll stay. Here I believe I could live. Oh, Heathcliff, I'm so afraid of death. Give me life.

HEATHCLIFF. *(Embracing her)* We'll make up for all we've lost.

CATHERINE. I wonder— *(A pause; gaily)* But of course we will. I'll even throw away my pretty dresses and be just as I used to be. *(Turning to window)* That is, I'll throw away all but one or two of the nicest. Look how our old heath rolls away. *It* never changes, does it? It must have been the same since the world began. Give me your hand.

HEATHCLIFF. *(Taking her hand)* Cathy—

(The LIGHT deepens as a cloud passes over the sun.)

CATHERINE. Ah, the sun is gone! What a pity! This morning one would never have thought it was going to storm. *(Shivering)* See how quickly the clouds are rising.

HEATHCLIFF. Let them!

CATHERINE. Yes—Wuthering was named for the storm, wasn't it? Oh, Heathcliff—

HEATHCLIFF. Cathy—

CATHERINE. Heathcliff—the wind—our sky and hills—all mingled in one bitter whirl of wind—

(They stand, the WIND blowing in their faces.)

ELLEN. *(Enters up Left.* ELLEN'S *voice is cold and unsympathetic)* Your husband is coming.

CATHERINE. *(Scarcely comprehending)* Oh! *(She glances out of the window.)*

ELLEN. You know you can't see from there. The mound hides the road. But I have seen. Ah, someone will pay for this day. Poor Master Linton!

HEATHCLIFF. *(Scornfully)* Poor Linton!

ELLEN. *(Coldly)* Yes. How frantic he must be— and how cruelly he is deceived!

HEATHCLIFF. *(Crossing toward* ELLEN*)* Save your pity.

CATHERINE. *(Following. Imploringly)* Heathcliff.

ELLEN. Well, at least there's a carriage to take you home.

HEATHCLIFF. She'll need no carriage, Ellen.

ELLEN. *(Startled)* Need no carriage!

CATHERINE. *(To* HEATHCLIFF*)* Must we tell him —now?

HEATHCLIFF. Yes.

CATHERINE. Yes—of course—

HEATHCLIFF. You're afraid?

CATHERINE. No—

HEATHCLIFF. Then why do you hesitate?

CATHERINE. Don't you understand? I only want to be kind. He loves me too. And Edgar's so proud —I don't want to hurt him. If you really love me you'll leave Edgar alone—you won't taunt him. Oh, Heathcliff, we mustn't build our love on hate—if we do it will destroy us!

ELLEN. *(Above sofa)* Catherine—you're not going to do this wicked thing— The very thought is—

(The door up Left bursts open. ISABEL *and* EDGAR, *both flushed and excited, enter.)*

ISABEL. *(Vindictively)* There! There she is—just as I said!

EDGAR. *(Hurrying to* CATHERINE's *side)* Catherine, love, how could you do such a thing? Ellen, did you know she was coming here?

CATHERINE. Ellen had nothing to do with it. I came of my own free will.

EDGAR. Have you no regard for me?

CATHERINE. I'm sorry, Edgar.

EDGAR. Come, Ellen, we'll take her home at once. Doctor Kenneth will be waiting for us.

HEATHCLIFF. One moment, Linton!

EDGAR. I have nothing to say to you, sir.

HEATHCLIFF. I have a great deal to say to you.

CATHERINE. Heathcliff, don't. I beg you. Let me tell him. It's I who must tell him.

EDGAR. Tell me—what?

CATHERINE. Oh, Edgar, try to understand—I'm not going back to the Grange.

EDGAR. Not going back—

CATHERINE. I can't go with you, Edgar. I must stay here—with Heathcliff.

ISABEL. *(Moving down Right)* I knew you intended to betray us.

EDGAR. Catherine, you can't mean what you say.

CATHERINE. I do mean it. I'm not coming with you, Edgar. I've always loved Heathcliff. I'm sorry I married you and I'm sorry I've made you unhappy, but now it's over and you must try to forgive.

ISABEL. All over indeed! And what of me? Have I nothing to say?

EDGAR. *(Recovering himself)* Leave this to me, Isabel. Of course, anyone can see she's out of her mind. She's sick—she doesn't even know what she's saying.

CATHERINE. Oh, Edgar, won't you face the truth for once? I'm not sick—at last I'm well again. At last I'm alive.

ELLEN. *(To EDGAR)* I'm afraid nothing you can say will change her wickedness, sir.

CATHERINE. Can't you understand, Edgar? Heathcliff and I love each other—we've loved each other since we were children.

ISABEL. I've always known it.

EDGAR. I'll never believe it—and I'll never let you go.

HEATHCLIFF. *(Crossing to EDGAR)* Yes, you will. You'll let her go because you can't hold her against me.

CATHERINE. Heathcliff!

ISABEL. And what are you but a brute, an animal!

HEATHCLIFF. It may be I am, but I'm through being cowed by weaklings whose life I could stop with my fingers.

(HEATHCLIFF *draws* EDGAR *toward him.* EDGAR *is paralyzed with fear.* ISABEL *and* ELLEN *cry out in terror.)*

ELLEN. Heathcliff—take care!

HEATHCLIFF. *(Oblivious to ALL but EDGAR)* I've always hated you.

EDGAR. Let me go.

HEATHCLIFF. *(Forcing EDGAR upstage Right)* I took your sister, but that didn't hurt you. Well, today I take your wife. *(Forcing EDGAR to his knees)* Now can you feel my strength—can you feel it now?

CATHERINE. *(Agonized)* Heathcliff—is that the

reason you want me? Oh, God—is there nothing but
hate? Are you going to kill our love—are you going
to kill—?

(A pause, then CATHERINE *falls.* ELLEN *cries out
and sinks on her knees beside* CATHERINE.
HEATHCLIFF *releases* EDGAR. *There is a deathly
silence during which* ISABEL *and* EDGAR *draw
together. At first* HEATHCLIFF *is too stunned to
move.* ELLEN *drops* CATHERINE'S *limp hand
and turns away weeping.)*

HEATHCLIFF. *(Kneeling beside* CATHERINE)
Cathy! Cathy! Answer me! *(A pause.)*
ELLEN. *(Her voice choked with grief and hatred)*
She'll not answer you now.
                          (WARN Curtain.)
ISABEL. *(Hysterically)* Oh, Edgar, Edgar!
EDGAR. It was God's will.
HEATHCLIFF. God's will! Then God's on your
side! (EDGAR *moves to touch* CATHERINE.) Don't
touch her—touch her and I'll kill you—I swear it.
EDGAR. But she's—
HEATHCLIFF. *(Guarding* CATHERINE—*savagely)*
She's mine—mine! No one shall touch her. Touch
her and I'll kill you.
EDGAR. *(Drawing back in horror)* Come, Isabel—
come at once—he's mad.
ISABEL. Heathcliff—

(HEATHCLIFF *does not hear.)*

EDGAR. Come with me, I say.

(ISABEL *and* EDGAR *go out Right.* ELLEN *shudders
and gathers up her cloak from sofa.)*

HEATHCLIFF. *(Blankly)* Ellen—

ELLEN. *(Above* HEATHCLIFF*)* What?

HEATHCLIFF. You're going?

ELLEN. Yes. I'll not stay longer here. Joseph was right—Wuthering is a house of death, with you its evil spirit.

HEATHCLIFF. Ellen—

ELLEN. *(A step toward* HEATHCLIFF*)* It was you who killed her! *(Sobbing)* You killed my little Catherine. *(At the Right door; hysterically)* Oh, let me go—let me out!

(ELLEN *goes. There is a pause.* HEATHCLIFF *bends quietly over* CATHERINE.)

HEATHCLIFF. Don't leave me, Cathy! Haunt me! They say the dead do haunt their murderers. Haunt me, then! Be with me always—take any form—drive me mad—but don't leave me alone—not alone—

CURTAIN

THE END

WUTHERING HEIGHTS

PROPERTY PLOT

ACT I

Right:
    Great armchair.
    Chair.
    Table-bench.
    Chair.

Center:
    Chair.
    Table.

Left:
    Settle.
    Firestool, andirons, etc.
    Wash-stand.
    Stool.

Off Right:
    Logs (JOSEPH).
    Awl and pieces of leather (HEATHCLIFF).
    Bucket (off; for water).
    Wind, thunder machines, lightning effect.

Center:
    Food on tray (table Center).
    Tablecloth, 2 plates, 2 glasses, 2 mugs, 2
        spoons.

Off Left:
    Tray, with supper covered by napkin.

Second tray, with plate of ham and bowl of
    pudding.
Bible (JOSEPH).
Dust cloth.

On Left:

Brandy bottle (mantel).
Mirror (on mantel).
Almanac (above mantel).
Clock (above mantel).
Knitting and bag (on settle).
Three pillows and mat (settle).
Bowl of apples (on settle).
Bed warmer (niche Left).
On washstand: Comb, bowl, towel, soap.
Pot, with water, near washstand.
Cabinet (in kitchen).

On Right:

Candelabra, candles, tapers (table).
Flowers.

ACT II

SCENE I

Right:

Chair.
Drum table.
Chair.

Center:

Console.
3 Chairs around tea table.
Stool.

Left:

Table.
Sofa.
Queen Anne chair.
Sewing table.

Off Left:
　　Brass tray, with tea and water pots.
　　Sugar bowl.
　　2 Tapers.
　　Special torn pillow.
　　Note.
　　Bunch of flowers.
　　Dust cloth.
Off Up Right:
　　2 Tapers.
　　1 Candle.
On Right:
　On drum table:
　　Ruby candelabra, protectors, candles.
　　Silver vase, flowers.
　　Silhouette.
　　Yellow book (drum table).
On Left:
　On table behind sofa are:
　　Tapers.
　　Single candelabrum.
　　Candle.
　　Vase of flowers.
　　4 Books wrapped in brown paper (EDGAR).
　On sofa:
　　1 Pillow.
　Fireplace:
　　Tongs.
　　Andirons.
　　Kindling (in basket).
On Center:
　　2 Vases (on console).
　　Mirror (on console).
　　Taper, one candle.
　　Sewing, basket (CATHERINE).
　On tea table:
　　4 Doillies, 4 napkins, creamer, 4 cups, saucers,

spoons, plate of tarts, plate of scones, plate of cookies, knives, jam pot, jam spoon.

ACT II

Scene 2

Change all flowers.
Dust cloth on chair, Right.
Windows closed Left.
Note ready, off Left.

Place drum table more Center; strike tea table.

ACT II

Scene 3

Special pillow, torn, Right of sofa.
Candle, up Right, lit.
Bolt Center French window.

ACT III

Swing settle Left down a bit.
Washstand before settle, with writing paper, in sheets, inkwell and pen.
Several chairs overturned, the room generally unkept.
Bunch of flowers off Right (CATHERINE).

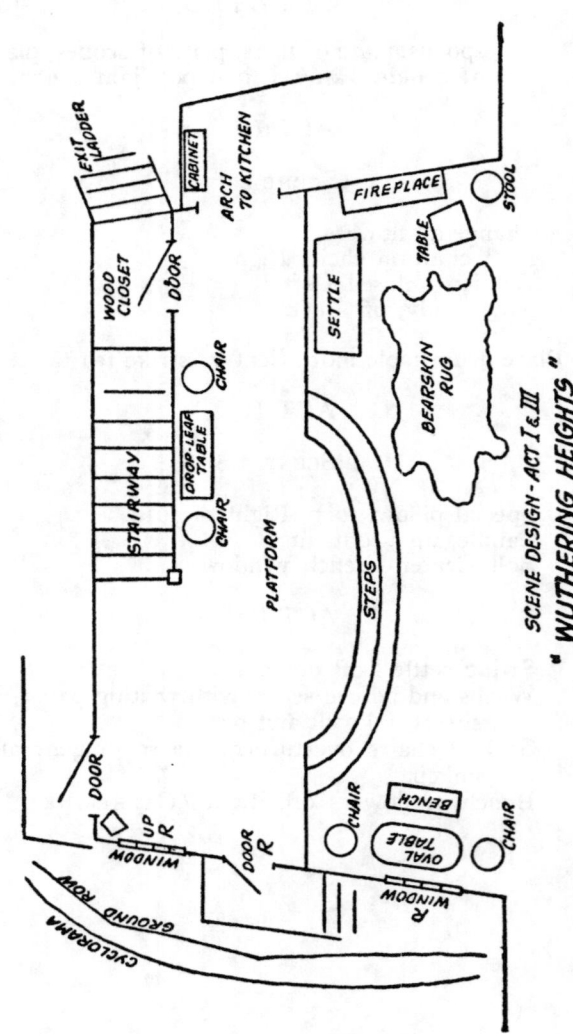

SCENE DESIGN - ACT I & III
" WUTHERING HEIGHTS "

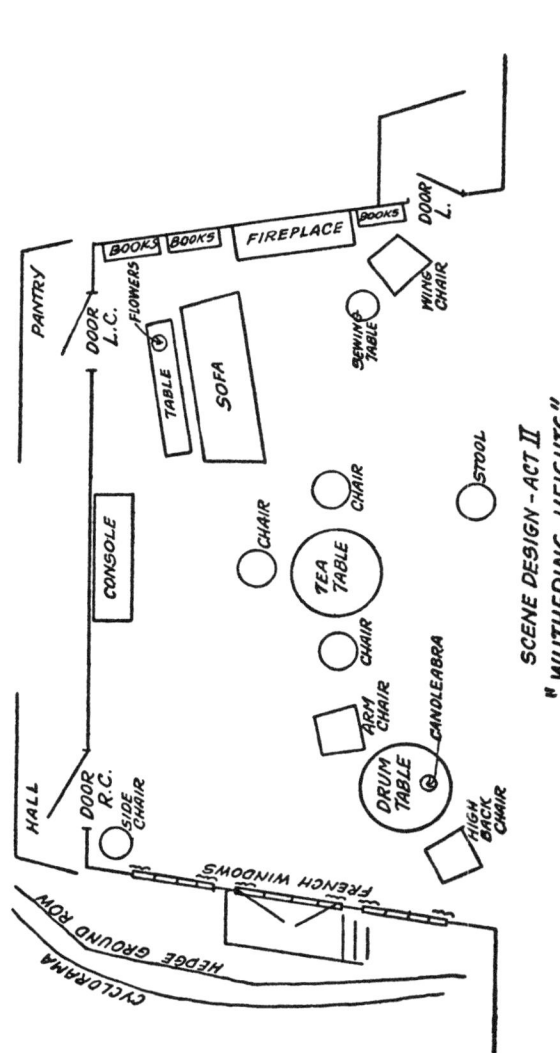

SCENE DESIGN – ACT II
"WUTHERING HEIGHTS"